# EDITED BY MIKE ROYSTON

Tales with a TWIST

## A NEW WINDMILL BOOK OF SHORT STORIES

Heinemann
*New Windmills*

Heinemann is an imprint of Pearson Education Limited,
a company incorporated in England and Wales, having
its registered office at Edinburgh Gate, Harlow, Essex, CM20 2JE.
Registered company number: 872828

Heinemann is a registered trademark of Pearson Education Limited

21

ISBN: 978 0 435 12513 4

Acknowledgements
The Editor and Publishers would like to thank the following for permission to use
copyright material:

Patrick Bone for 'The Secret of City Cemetery' by Patrick Bone, from *Bruce Colville's Book of
Ghosts*. Used with the kind permission of the author; HarperCollins Publishers Ltd for 'Even
Stevens FC' by Michael Rosen from *The Young Oxford Book of Football Stories*, ed. James
Riordan, published by OUP, 1998; Penguin Books Australia Ltd for 'Smart Ice-Cream' from
*Unreal*, by Paul Jennings, published by Penguin Books Australia Ltd; A P Watt Ltd on behalf of
Dick King-Smith for 'Just a Guess' by Dick King-Smith from *The Methuen Book of Strange Tales*,
1980; Maggie Powell for 'An Alien Stole My Brain', © Maggie Powell; © 1996 Vivian Richardson.
Extracted from *Riding the Silver Wave* by Ben Bo, published by Doubleday 1996, a division of
Transworld Publishers. All rights reserved; David Higham Associates for 'Man from the South' by
Roald Dahl from *The Puffin Book of Horror Stories*, ed. Andrew Horowitz, published by Pufin,
1996; The Library Association for 'Karate for Kids' by Terence Blacker from *Stacks of Stories*, ed.
Mary Hoffman, published by Hodder, 1997; The Orion Publishing Group Ltd for 'Gone Fishing'
by Jean Richardson from *Scared Stiff*, ed. Wendy Cooling, published by Orion Children's Books;
The Agency (London) Ltd for 'Dan, Dan the Half-Time Man' © Janet Burchett and Sara Vogler
1998, first published by Corgi (Transworld) 1998 in *Football Fever 2*, ed. Tony Bradman. All
rights reserved and enquiries to The Agency (London) Ltd, 24 Pottery Lane, London, W11 4LZ,
fax: 0171 7279037; The Orion Publishing Group Ltd for 'The Amazing Mr Endicott' from *Dare
You*, ed. Wendy Cooling, published by Orion Children's Books.

The Publishers have made every effort to trace the copyright holders, but if they have
inadvertently overlooked any, they will be pleased to make the necessary arrangements at
the first opportunity.

Cover design by The Point
Cover illustration by Rob Hefferan
Illustrations by Jackie Hill at 320 Design; 'The Secret of City Cemetery' – Neil Parker;
'Even Stevens' – Bob Wilson; 'Smart Ice-Cream' – Bob Wilson; 'Just a Guess' – Phillip Bannister;
'An Alien Stole My Brain' – M H Jeeves; 'Riding the Silver Wave' – Phillip Bannister;
'Man from the South' – Hashim Akib; 'Karate for Kids' – M H Jeeves;
'Gone Fishing' – David Hopkins; 'Dan, Dan the Half-Time Man' – Neil Parker;
'The Amazing Mr Endicott' – Hashim Akib.
Typeset by ⚒ Tek-Art Croydon Surrey

Printed in China (CTPS/21)

# Contents

**Introduction**                                                    **v**

*The Secret of City Cemetery* – Patrick Bone                         1

*Even Stevens FC* – Michael Rosen                                    7

*Smart Ice-Cream* – Paul Jennings                                   23

*Just a Guess* – Dick King-Smith                                    28

*An Alien Stole My Brain* – Maggie Powell                           41

*Riding the Silver Wave* – Ben Bo                                   49

*Man from the South* – Roald Dahl                                   61

*Karate for Kids* – Terence Blacker                                 75

*Gone Fishing* – Jean Richardson                                    85

*Dan, Dan the Half-Time Man* – Janet Burchett
and Sara Vogler                                                     96

*The Amazing Mr Endicott* – Eric Brown                            108

**Activities**                                                    **119**

# Introduction

With some stories, you know what's likely to happen after the first page. Good story-writers, on the other hand, keep you wondering: 'How will it all turn out?' They always have a surprise or two up their sleeves.

Each of the *Tales with a Twist* in this book has been chosen to surprise you – especially at the end. Teenage readers helped do the choosing. All the stories were put through the Twist Test by pupils of your age. It worked. No one stopped reading half-way through.

You will find these stories surprising in other ways, too. They are all about unusual situations. A weekend football team ends up playing in a Wembley Cup Final. A practical joker finds himself trapped in an open grave during a burial. A teenage boy goes on a fishing trip with two friends who died over a century ago. How?

The writers in this book invite you to let your imagination run wild. What would *you* do if you woke up to discover a creature from another planet had invaded your mind? How can a 100-year-old man be the link between a colony of aliens and a schoolboy? Glance at the Contents Page and work out which stories might give you the answers.

It's not that the things described in these stories *couldn't* happen. Just that it would be unlikely. Still, you never can tell . . .

Enjoy them.

*Mike Royston*

# The Secret of City Cemetery
## Patrick Bone

Only kids believed City Cemetery was haunted. But that changed the Hallowe'en night fourteen-year-old Willard Armbruster disappeared. His body was never found.

Willard was a bully. He had no friends. There wasn't a kid in school who would play with him. But Willard didn't mind. He liked being a bully. The older he grew, the better he became at it.

Once, he told Wylma Jean Kist that her mother had been run over by a subway train. It took Wylma Jean weeks to get over Willard's *joke*. That didn't bother Willard. It just made him want to invent meaner pranks to play on people.

That's why he was beside himself with glee when he saw city workmen digging graves at the edge of the public cemetery. They were paupers' graves, intended for persons whose families couldn't afford the fancy plots near the centre of the cemetery. Several graves were dug before winter frost would make digging difficult. Willard knew they would be filled in as needed.

He was clever enough to see that the part of the cemetery where the graves had been dug was located next to the playground of Mark Twain Middle School. The sidewalk leading into the school playground and up to the front entrance ran beside the freshly-dug graves. There was no way a kid could go in or out of the playground or school building without passing by the graves.

When weather permitted, smaller neighbourhood children always played in the schoolyard till dark. Willard didn't believe in ghosts. But he knew most of the kids did. He counted on that.

One evening, just before dark, he snuck into the graveyard next to where some kids were playing catch on the school playground. Fall had set in, and the days were growing darker. Willard hid near the freshly-dug graves. At sunset the kids started to leave. Dark clouds hovered overhead. Wind whistled eerily through the trees.

'Perfect!' he snickered as he lowered himself into one of the graves, using a small stepladder he had stolen for the occasion. As the kids walked near the graves, he moaned in a pathetic, pleading voice, 'Help me! I'm still alive! Nooo, nooo. I'm alive! Please help me!'

The kids screamed all the way home, where they told their parents that someone was buried 'alive' in one of the graves.

At first none of the parents took them seriously.

'Ghost stories,' they all agreed. 'Overactive imagination,' some said. But when Willard played the trick again, a few parents called the police. Willard was long gone when they went out to check. After a while no one paid any attention to the kids. Police stopped checking, and the students at Mark Twain got used to the trick. They decided no one was actually buried alive. It was the ghost's way of haunting them from the graveyard.

Willard had fooled everyone. At least, that's what he thought.

One evening just before the cemetery closed, Henry Grasmick, the graveyard caretaker, saw Willard sneaking into the cemetery again. Henry always ignored the occasional kid who ran in and out of the graveyard to tempt the ghost and brag about it. But what Willard had been doing was not only tempting, it was cruel. So Henry crept up behind Willard and whispered, 'I know what you're up to, boy.'

Willard jumped as if a spider had crawled up his pants. When he saw it was Henry, he didn't act as if he was

afraid. 'Get away from me, you ugly old man,' he said, and spat right at Henry's shoes.

Henry wasn't intimidated. 'You don't know what you're getting into, boy. It ain't no good to mess with the ghost.'

Willard laughed. 'What ghost? I never saw any ghost. Even if one does exist, he can't do anything to me. Ghosts are spirits, old man. They can't touch me. But I can touch you' – he raised his fist – 'which is exactly what I'll do if you snitch on me!'

Henry ignored the threat. 'Don't mess with the ghost,' he repeated. 'He does exist. He has his ways. Since I was a boy I worked here, and he left me alone. But I never messed with him.' Henry turned as if he were about to leave. 'You don't have to worry about me telling on you, young man. You only have to worry about what the ghost is going to do to you if you keep coming here.'

Henry's warning had some effect, because Willard did stop his tricks at the cemetery for a time. But he stayed busy elsewhere.

He almost got away with some vandalism at school, but became too sure of himself and was caught and placed on a week's detention. He got bored. On his last day of detention he flushed a cherry bomb down a third-floor toilet, shattering the commodes on every floor below. School psychologists had to be called in to counsel the kids who happened to be sitting on the pots when they exploded.

Willard was proud of his pranks, but he could never forget the excitement of playing dead in an open grave. He was soon to get the thrill of his life.

Hallowe'en night the middle school had a haunted house. To Willard, that meant one thing. Most of the kids would be there. He was delighted. Everyone who came would have to walk down the path past the open graves. *No more small-time tricks*, he thought to himself. *This time I scare all the kids*.

He arrived early at the cemetery and lowered himself into one of the graves, staying low so no one would see him. He even put his stepladder on the ground under him to make sure it was out of sight.

The sun set. Willard watched the darkness close over his grave like a shroud. He shivered and cursed the cold. It had rained earlier. He smelled the mouldy mud squishing under his feet. Suddenly he heard footsteps. He was about to scream out, 'Help me! I'm still alive!' But he realized the footsteps were coming from *inside* the cemetery, and not *outside*, on the children's path.

He froze, not from the night chill.

*Is it the police*, he thought, *or someone else who has discovered the tricks I've been playing?*

Now *he* was afraid, and the fear of being discovered was more than he could take. So he huddled there, as far down in the grave as he could, hoping whoever it was would go away without finding him. But the footsteps didn't go away. They got louder, and closer.

*Maybe it isn't the police*, he thought. *Maybe it isn't . . . even human? Or maybe . . .* He didn't want to consider that maybe he had gone too far in mocking the dead.

In his mind Willard could hear the old caretaker's warning: *'Don't mess with the ghost, boy. The ghost has his ways.'*

The footsteps were closer now. They were heavy steps. Soon Willard realized there were several sets of footsteps, coming directly to his grave. He was too terrified to scream. All he could do was stare up at the mouth of the grave and wait. Suddenly, just above the grave, he heard groans, heavy breathing, shuffling, and grunting sounds.

That's when he saw it. Something long and large and black hovered over him, then inched towards him into the grave.

It took Willard a split second to realize *It's a coffin!* and less than that to scream, 'No! Please! I'm down here!'

All four gravediggers reacted the same way. They dropped the ropes holding the coffin and ran for help. The coffin fell like dead weight, directly on Willard – *thump* – knocking him cold.

Minutes later the cemetery superintendent showed up with the gravediggers to inspect the grave.

'There's nothing down there but a coffin,' he said. 'Boys, I ain't got time for ghost stories. The only spirits in this graveyard are the ones you've been drinking. Now, why don't you just bury that body.'

When Willard came to, he discovered the 'trick' was on him.

Every Hallowe'en since, school children have claimed they could hear the muffled screams of the Ghost of City Cemetery, begging to be released.

'Help me! Please help me, I'm alive! Noooo, noooo. I'm alive! Pleeease! Don't leave me here!'

# Even Stevens FC
## Michael Rosen

Wayne Travis was football mad. So were most of his friends. Every day after school, they played 23-a-side football in the space round by the dustbins. No ref. One goal.

Wayne's ambition was to be a professional footballer. Every day he watched his *Goals of the Century* video and imagined being on television.

Wayne's other ambition was to perfect the famous Hedley Carlton Triple-Bounce Goal, as described to him by his grandad:

'I shall never forget that goal. It wasn't just the swerve; it wasn't just the speed; each bounce zigzagged across the pitch as if the ball had a life of its own.'

Wayne decided to have a go. His foot swerved as it approached the ball, then spun back the other way. At the same time it flipped up under the ball.

The result was amazing. The ball flew like a rocket towards Shaheed. It dipped, bounced, swerved off towards Roger and Harry. It bounced again and swerved back towards the two Shonas.

It bounced again and headed for Maxine and Lara.

Then it hurtled into the goal, hitting the wall with a thunderous wham.

From then on, Wayne practised the foot move whenever he could. Under the table, on the bus, at breakfast . . . swerve, spin-back, flip-up; swerve, spin-back, flip-up.

Wayne wasn't the only one in his family who liked football. On Saturday mornings Wayne's dad played for a team called Even Stevens.

Everyone in the team lived in Shakespeare Street. It was called Even Stevens because all the players lived in houses or flats with even numbers. They played their matches on the Astroturf behind the Mammoth Hypermarket.

## EVEN STEVENS FC
### *Team Notes*
(nicknames in brackets)

*Erkan Hussein*, 21. Leather worker. Excellent right foot, terrible left. Mother works at Tesco. (*Tesco*)

*Harry Postlethwaite*, 52. Bus driver. Terrible right foot, terrible left foot. Says he knew Sir Stanley Matthews. (*Stan*)

*Darren Stewart*, 13. School kid. Brilliant all-rounder. Only one eye. (*Nelson*)

*Chuck Bradley*, 35. Unemployed. Ex-American football player. (*Superbowl*)

*Moira Stewart*, 41. Darren's mum, ex-Scotland ladies team. (*Jock*)

*Satoshi Watanabe*, 20. Student. Broke Tokyo record for spinning a basketball on one finger. (*Guinness*)

*Solly Rosenberg*, 68. Once captained United London Jewish Boys' Club's tour of Wales. (*Taffy*)

*Linton Harper*, 19. Computer salesman. Rap artist, team kit style consultant. Wikkid! (*Mr Kool*)

*Linford Harper*, 21. Linton's older brother. Bosses him around something shocking. (*Bossman*)

*Nigel Fiddle*, 18. Shoe shop assistant. Awful player, but can get football boots dead cheap. (*Start-rite*)

*Rodney Travis*, 38. Wayne's dad. Bad back, bad right knee, bad shoulder, bad neck. Part-time postman. (*Pat*)

*Salvatore Delgado*, 16. Claims to be grandson of reserve team member in 1970 World Cup-winning Brazil squad. (*Pelé*)

*Donna Louis*, 16. Ex-spectator of Linton. Now plays in own right. (*Mrs Kool*)

One Friday night in September, Erkan called round to see Wayne's dad.

'Guess what, Pat, we're eligible for the FA Cup. The draw's just come through and we're up against Wealdstone next Saturday!'

'Wealdstone?' said Wayne's dad. 'But they're a really brilliant side, with ex-professionals. We'll be smashed.'

Erkan wasn't put off. He told all the members of the team the good news. But there were a few problems.

For one thing, Nigel Fiddle was in Latvia buying a stock of cheap shoes, so he wouldn't be able to play. For another, Wayne's dad now had a bad left knee, so he wouldn't be able to play either.

Undaunted, that Saturday Erkan led Even Stevens FC out to play Wealdstone on the Astroturf behind the Mammoth Hypermarket.

And in that team was young Wayne Travis.

For everyone in Shakespeare Street it was a huge thrill, but no one else took much notice, except for a woman from the local radio station who happened to be passing.

'Wealdstone's attack has been kept at bay by some extraordinary long-ball bouncing passes by young Wayne Travis. They've just conceded a penalty in the eighty-ninth minute. Thirteen-year-old Darren Stewart is taking the kick. He runs up . . . It's a goal! And there's the final whistle! Wealdstone have been beaten in the first qualifying round of the FA Cup!'

It turned out to be the scoop of the year for local radio.

Back in the dressing room (Moira Stewart's front room) Darren explained, 'The goalie was watching my face and not the ball. So I leered at him with my false eye and he went the wrong way.'

The next day, Wayne and the rest of the team tuned in to the local radio to hear the draw for the next round:

'  . . . versus Hendon. Bishop Auckland versus Corinthian Casuals. Cartilege United versus Even Stevens. Pinner versus . . . '

'Yeees!' yelled Darren. 'Cartilege United! Didn't we beat them 4–nil only a few months back?'

Meanwhile, in a garden shed somewhere in Enfield, Cartilege United were not so happy . . .

'Oh no, Even Stevens. That really does it.'

'Sorry, I can't make September 28th. I've got to mow the lawn.'

'My brother's giving me a haircut that day.'

'I've got to take the mower over to Uncle Bill's.'

'Yeah, me too, Dad.'

And so Even Stevens didn't have to play anyone at all in the next round of the FA Cup!

Successfully through the qualifying rounds, their next challenge was to play the non-league professionals. They were drawn away against the powerful Telford United. As the *Hackney Mercury* put it (in its 'On the Ball' column by Chris Hack):

---

Young Wayne Travis is on top of the world. Just 9 years old, he's in the country's greatest football tournament.

'It's brill,' states Wayne from his home in Shakespeare Street. 'His mum would've been proud of him,' adds Dad Rodney (38) part-time postman and widower.

And what of the amazing long-ball triple-bouncing passes we saw in the game?

'Just a fluke,' says fair-haired Wayne. 'I don't want to make too much of it.'

But it's certainly a RED LETTER day for Postman Dad!!!

When the big day came, Wayne's dad's knees were still playing up and Nigel was still in Latvia (or was it Poland?). So Wayne was in the team.

On the coach to Telford, Erkan dished out advice.

'I want commitment. Hard tackling in mid-field, early ball to Jock and Nelson up front. Zigzag (Wayne now had his own nickname, thanks to the Hedley Carlton Triple-Bounce), I want you to cover Taffy when he gets tired and only use that tricky long-ball bounce-pass when there's space down the middle.'

On the way to the game, the team sang songs in their coach:

'Even Stevens is the name,
We're the best in the game,
We're the best in the west,
We're the best of the rest.'

On the way back from Telford . . .

'I haven't seen a match like that since the 1953 Cup Final when Stanley Matthews beat Bolton Wanderers single-handed.'

'Zigzag's passing was amazing.'

'But who got the winning touchdown, guys?'

'We call it a goal, Superbowl.'

By the time the coach got back to Hackney, the crowds were out to welcome them.

'There's only one Wayne Travis,
There's only one Wayne Travis.'

'Su-per, super bowl,
Su-per, super bowl.'

'Mrs Kool
Mrs Kool,
Mrs, Mrs Kool,
She's got long hair,

And she don't care,
Mrs, Mrs Kool.'

Next day, the draw for the first round of the FA Cup took place on TV.

'Even Stevens versus Blackpool . . .'

Old Harry Postlethwaite couldn't believe his ears.

'I don't believe it! That's Stanley Matthews' old team. When we beat . . .'

'Bolton Wanderers single-handed in the 1953 Cup Final!' chorused his family.

'Will I get to play?' wondered Wayne.

He needn't have worried.

'We need you, Zigzag,' shouted Satoshi. 'No one can read your game.'

The Astroturf at the back of the Mammoth Hypermarket had never known anything like it. The car park was converted into a terrace and the local printer was selling programmes.

---

**EVEN STEVENS**
**Official programme**
*Price 50p*
Even Stevens v Blackpool FC
*(featuring Wayne 'Zigzag' Travis)*
**FA CUP FIRST ROUND**

---

Every child and teacher from Wayne's school was there – even the head. The whole nation tuned in to hear the report at the end of Grandstand.

'Two seconds into the game and the non-leaguers were 1–nil down. It appeared to be a walk-over for the one-time Cup-winning club of the great Sir Stanley Matthews. But how that mighty name suffered today, as Blackpool experienced four early send-offs for unclean tackling!

'With Blackpool down to seven men, Even Stevens were in with a chance. But Blackpool had further surprises in store, when four forwards formed a rugby scrum and charged towards the goal with the ball tucked under one of the jerseys. Early bath for them too, and Blackpool were down to three men.

'Even Stevens equalized after half-time. And then, in what must be one of the upsets of the century, young Wayne Travis took control of the ball.

'Kicked from well outside Blackpool's penalty area, the ball made an astonishing triple-bouncing journey up the pitch. I couldn't really see from where I was, but somehow or other it landed up in the Blackpool net.

'At the final whistle it was 2–1 to Even Stevens. They're into round two, and they'll be celebrating down in Hackney tonight, I can tell you.'

That night was the greatest night of Wayne's life and he ate two kebabs, fourteen jaffa cakes, four Jamaican patties, eight slices of celebration cake, fourteen packets of crisps, and twelve chocolate bars at the celebration party in Shakespeare Street

The next draw turned out to be against non-league Waterloo Station Rovers – what a let-down! It would have been much more fun to be beaten by one of the league teams.

Wayne went back to playing 23-a-side football in the alley behind school. He didn't practise his Hedley Carlton Triple-Bounce Goal.

A few weeks later, while Wayne was doing his homework and Dad was dozing in his armchair . . .

'. . . Semi-professional football club, Waterloo Station Rovers, has been forced to close down . . . in a statement . . . fraud . . . fifty thousand pounds missing . . . in court tomorrow . . . punched the manager . . . police . . . no further part in the FA Cup.'

Wayne's dad work up and leapt to his feet so suddenly that he put his back out.

'That means we're through the second round of the FA Cup! If only I could get myself fit in time.'

At first Wayne thought – brilliant! Playing one of the big boys. But then he thought, What if Dad *does* get fit in time?

Wouldn't that mean he'd lose his place in the team? And hadn't Nigel Fiddle rung from Poland (or Bulgaria) the other day to say he was on his way back with a lorry load of new shoes and boots?

When Even Stevens were drawn away against Manchester United in the third round, even Moira Stewart was stunned to silence.

Manchester United?

Old Trafford?

A crowd of over forty thousand?

Live coverage on TV?

Maybe they should simply bow out now before nerves and humiliation got the better of them. Instead, what happened was one of the most curious and extraordinary games of football in the world.

Erkan Hussein may not have been the world's greatest captain, but he knew a thing or two about football. In the weeks leading up to the game he racked his brains and, by the day of the Big Match, he had a plan.

In the dressing room at Old Trafford he revealed it for the first time. (He drew it in the steam on the dressing room window.)

As the teams ran out on to the pitch, the roar that hit them nearly knocked Wayne over. He was on the subs bench today, next to his dad who had a bad toe. (Nigel, who was back from Romania, had said, 'Either I play or you lot don't get the new boots.')

Then came the Erkan Hussein plan.

'. . . an amazing sight here at Old Trafford. The non-leaguers are in a semi-circle guarding their own goal. The United forwards are trying to fight their way through but there really is no way round this.

'Man. United's captain has called a conference . . .

'. . . And Even Stevens have broken out of the semi-circle. They're taking the ball upfield . . . and they've scored! And Man. United haven't even noticed. What an amazing move!'

And 1–nil was where the score stayed until the final whistle. One of the smallest clubs in the world had beaten one of the biggest.

That night the World Football Council had an emergency meeting in the Eiffel Tower and changed the rules of football so that it could never happen again:

*Rule Number 457*
Semi circles and defences.
Teams are not allowed to form a defensive ring round the goal.

Even Stevens were through to Round 4, away to Bristol Rovers. It was never going to be an easy game after the scandal at Old Trafford. The *SCUM* paper wrote,

---

Even Cheaters
CHEATS!!!
Dirty, cheating crooks, Even Stevens, go to Bristol today and let's hope they get well and truly crushed.
BEAT THE CHEATS!!!

---

'Look at this, Dad,' cried Wayne.

'Football's a cruel game, son,' said Dad.

But Wayne was back in the team. (Nigel Fiddle had to go back to Romania – or was it Estonia? He had forgotten to pick up the bootlaces.)

Two minutes into the game, Bristol's Jimmy Rack left the field.

'Bristol Rovers will not be fielding any substitutes today: David Dover's wife, Eileen, has gone into hospital to have a baby and David's with her. Best of luck, Eileen! And – amazing coincidence – Doug Bitnearer's wife is having a baby too – best of luck, Lena!'

Three minutes later, three more went . . .

'Well, here's a turn-up for the books. Jimmy Rack's missus, Anna, has just been taken to hospital. They're expecting their third child. Best of luck, Anna!'

One minute later . . .

'Dennis Pond's wife, Lily, George Showers's wife, April, and Pete Bee's wife, May, have all just been taken to hospital to have their babies.

'Well, there's certainly going to be a few more little Rovers in town tonight. Good luck Laura Norder, Ruby Redd and the rest . . . !'

Bristol Rovers were down to one man. Even Stevens won 45–nil.

Even Stevens were through to the fifth round of the FA Cup, with only sixteen clubs left in. Life was supposed to go on as usual for the players, but it wasn't easy.

Erkan's leather factory started making leather badges:

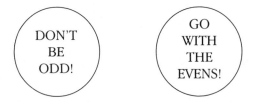

Satoshi regularly appeared on satellite TV to Japan.

Linton was Number 1 in the Rap Charts with 'Believin' Even Stevens'.

And Wayne . . . ? Well, the whole school was doing a project on football.

Even Stevens featured in the papers almost every day.

---

SCUMsport
FA CUP FIFTH ROUND
Win the pools with Harry Bigforest
WIMBLEDON v. EVEN STEVENS
This should be a pushover for Wimbledon. Their superior long ball game should easily penetrate the non-leaguers' defence, though Stevens' captain, 'Tesco' Hussein, tells me he's got something special up his sleeve (and it's not just his arm).

---

And indeed he had. When Even Stevens ran out on to the pitch for the game, everything looked normal. But the moment the whistle blew, Even Stevens turned their backs on the Wimbledon goal and played the whole game running backwards.

Wimbledon's Great Walnut tackled Moira.

The ref blew him up for tackling from behind.

Ron Cobnut tackled Donna.

The ref blew him up for tackling from behind.

It was unbeatable. Wimbledon were completely outplayed.

FINAL SCORE
Wimbledon 0, Even Stevens 3

That night the World Football Council had an emergency meeting at Niagara Falls:

*Rule Number 458*
Running backwards.

No team shall spend more than two minutes running, shooting, passing, or playing set-pieces backwards.

Even Stevens were through to the last eight.

Moira was a guest on breakfast television, and Linton appeared in a quiz show. Every single member of the team was involved in something, from opening supermarkets to charity work.

Wayne was finding it hard to concentrate in school. Some of his mates were really jealous.

'I'm better at football than you, Wayne. I ought to be playing for the Stevens.'

'Maybe you are, but you don't live at an even number in Shakespeare Street, do you? So, hard cheese!'

In the sixth round Even Stevens were drawn at home to Aston Villa.

Now, you probably would agree that Even Stevens had had a bit of luck so far in the tournament. But what happened next was unheard of in the history of football.

Aston Villa got lost. That's right, lost.

As Wayne told his dad, 'That's hard luck on the Villa fans, Dad.'

'Football's a cruel game, son,' said Dad.

They just couldn't find their way to the Mammoth Hypermarket Astroturf. Perhaps the trouble was that Mammoth were doing rather good business and had opened up twelve new stores between Aston Villa and Hackney, but whatever it was, Villa never made it to the match.

That night, the draw was made on TV.

'We're through to the semi-finals! Liverpool versus Even Stevens!'

Wayne was over the moon.

That week, Even Stevens trained hard. Erkan had run out of ideas and the intrepid team were just glad that they had lasted long enough to meet such brilliant opponents.

That week, Liverpool played hard. On Monday they played Bayern Munich in the fourth round of the European Cup. It was a draw, replay Thursday night.

On Tuesday they played in the fifth round of the Humbellow Cup. It was a draw, replay Friday night.

On Thursday they played in the replay of the fourth round of the European Cup. It went to extra time. They lost.

On Friday they played in the replay of the fifth round of the Humbellow Cup. It went to extra time. They lost.

Anyone could have beaten Liverpool that day.

Final score: Liverpool 0, Even Stevens 6.

'Isn't that . . .' began Wayne.

'Football's a cruel game, son,' said Dad.

Yes, the amazing news was that Even Stevens, the team from Shakespeare Street, Hackney, were in the FA Cup Final.

The bad news was that Nigel Fiddle was back from Lithuania with another lot of boots, and he wanted to play. Wayne's dad's back was finally on the mend, too. Things didn't look good for Wayne.

At last the great day arrived.

### THE FINAL

*4 mins*

'. . . Spurs launch an attack down the middle. Sparrow sprays it out on the right flank to Doddle. A beautiful cross; it's beaten Rodney Travis! Greyleg has run through to nod it in. 1–nil to Tottenham, but there was a suspicion of off-side. Let's look at it again on the replay . . . and yes, definitely offside . . . Bobby?'

'Absolutely.'

*22 mins*

'. . . Doddle jinxing his way round the Stevens' defence. Postlethwaite's got it back, and, oh, that's a foul, surely? Referee waves play on. Doddle takes it on the left foot. Top corner. It's a goal!! 2–nil to Tottenham. Let's look at that again on the replay . . . and yes, that's a foul, surely . . . Bobby?'

'Absolutely.'

*43 mins*

'Greyleg takes the corner, and it's Doddle with the diving header. Fantastic save by Bradley. No! The referee's given a goal!! Let's look at that again. Oh no, you can see Bradley held it. Oh dear me, the third controversial goal, Bobby . . .'

'Absolutely.'

Second half
*51 mins*

'. . . And Travis is down!'

*56 mins*

'. . . and Wayne Travis is on. Eyebulge towers over him, but Travis gets it away. Extraordinary – it's turning towards the penalty area. It's heading for goal. Speadeagle's got it covered . . . Oh, no he hasn't. It's in! It's a goal! That's 3–1 to Spurs. The pitch must be a little uneven today, Bobby?'

'Absolutely.'

*79 mins*

'. . . Donna Louis fairly steaming through mid-field there. Travis takes it. Oh, it's a tame one. Bounces early, takes a strange turn. Slug's covering – he's misjudged it. Greyleg will clear off the line, surely . . . No – it's in. It's a goal!! Sensational! 3–2.

'The referee ought to look at the stitching on the ball, don't you agree, Bobby?'

'Absolutely.'

The seconds were ticking away. The ref was looking at his watch. If only Wayne could get the ball once more.

'Give it to Zigzag!' came a shout.

As the ref put the whistle in his mouth, Satoshi slipped Wayne the ball.

Wayne took a huge swipe at it. Off it went. One bounce, two bounces, three bounces.

It was going to be a goal . . .

It was going to be the equalizer . . .

. . . Then the whistle went.

Half a second later the ball was in the net. Goal but no goal.

No extra time.

End of game.

Spurs had won the cup.

Then an odd thing happened. Instead of letting the losing team collect their medals, the Spurs captain ran up to collect the FA Cup. He brought it back down to the pitch and gave Erkan the lid.

'You were robbed, mate,' he said.

Everyone agreed it was the most extraordinary FA Cup Final in football history. People all over the world argued about the final score.

Wayne finally got his wish and appeared on the new *Goals of the Century* video.

And today people still study Wayne's kicks to see exactly what happened. The argument rages.

But Wayne Travis and the Even Stevens FC squad will never forget that day.

'You'd have beaten them with that Hedley Carlton Triple-Bounce, son, if you'd had the chance,' sighed Dad.

'Well . . .' said Wayne, 'football's a cruel game, Dad!'

# Smart Ice-Cream
## Paul Jennings

Well, I came top of the class again. One hundred out of one hundred for Maths. And one hundred out of one hundred for English. I'm just a natural brain, the best there is. There isn't one kid in the class who can come near me. Next to me they are all dumb.

Even when I was a baby I was smart. The day that I was born my mother started tickling me. 'Bub, bub, bub,' she said.

'Cut it out, Mum,' I told her. 'That tickles.' She nearly fell out of bed when I said that. I was very advanced for my age.

Every year I win a lot of prizes: top of the class, top of the school, stuff like that. I won a prize for spelling when I was only three years old. I am a terrific speller. If you can say it, I can spell it. Nobody can trick me on spelling. I can spell every word there is.

Some kids don't like me; I know that for a fact. They say I'm a show-off. I don't care. They are just jealous because they are not as clever as me. I'm good-looking too. That's another reason why they are jealous.

Last week something bad happened. Another kid got one hundred out of one hundred for Maths too. That never happened before – no one has ever done as well as me. I am always first on my own A kid called Jerome Dadian beat me. He must have cheated. I was sure he cheated. It had something to do with that ice-cream. I was sure of it. I decided to find out what was going on; I wasn't going to let anyone pull a fast one on me.

It all started with the ice-cream man, Mr Peppi. The old fool had a van which he parked outside the school. He sold ice-cream, all different types. He had every flavour there is, and some that I had never heard of before.

He didn't like me very much. He told me off once. 'Go to the back of the queue,' he said. 'You pushed in.'

'Mind your own business, Pop,' I told him. 'Just hand over the ice-cream.'

'No,' he said. 'I won't serve you unless you go to the back.'

I went round to the back of the van, but I didn't get in the queue. I took out a nail and made a long scratch on his rotten old van. He had just had it painted. Peppi came and had a look. Tears came into his eyes. 'You are a bad boy,' he said. 'One day you will get into trouble. You think you are smart. One day you will be too smart.'

I just laughed and walked off. I knew he wouldn't do anything. He was too soft-hearted. He was always giving free ice-creams to kids that had no money. He felt sorry for poor people. The silly fool.

There were a lot of stories going round about that ice-cream. People said that it was good for you. Some kids said that it made you better when you were sick. One of the teachers called it 'Happy Ice-Cream'. I didn't believe it; it never made me happy.

All the same, there was something strange about it. Take Pimples Peterson for example. That wasn't his real name – I just called him that because he had a lot of pimples. Anyway, Peppi heard me calling Peterson 'Pimples'. 'You are a real mean boy,' he said. 'You are always picking on someone else, just because they are not like you.'

'Get lost, Peppi,' I said. 'Go and flog your ice-cream somewhere else.'

Peppi didn't answer me. Instead he spoke to Pimples. 'Here, eat this,' he told him. He handed Peterson an ice-cream. It was the biggest ice-cream I had ever seen. It was coloured purple. Peterson wasn't too sure about it. He didn't think he had enough money for such a big ice-cream.

'Go on,' said Mr Peppi. 'Eat it. I am giving it to you for nothing. It will get rid of your pimples.'

I laughed and laughed. Ice-cream doesn't get rid of pimples, it *gives* you pimples. Anyway, the next day when Peterson came to school he had no pimples. Not one. I couldn't believe it. The ice-cream had cured his pimples.

There were some other strange things that happened too. There was a kid at the school who had a long nose. Boy, was it long. He looked like Pinocchio. When he blew it you could hear it a mile away. I called him 'Snozzle'. He didn't like being called Snozzle. He used to go red in the face when I said it, and that was every time that I saw him. He didn't say anything back – he was scared that I would punch him up.

Peppi felt sorry for Snozzle too. He gave him a small green ice-cream every morning, for nothing. What a jerk. He never gave me a free ice-cream.

You won't believe what happened but I swear it's true. Snozzle's nose began to grow smaller. Every day it grew a bit smaller. In the end it was just a normal nose. When it was the right size Peppi stopped giving him the green ice-creams.

I made up my mind to put a stop to this ice-cream business. Jerome Dadian had been eating ice-cream the day he got one hundred for Maths. It must have been the ice-cream making him smart. I wasn't going to have anyone doing as well as me. I was the smartest kid in the school, and that's the way I wanted it to stay. I wanted to get a look inside that ice-cream van to find out what was going on.

I knew where Peppi kept his van at night – he left it in a small lane behind his house. I waited until about eleven o'clock at night. Then I crept out of the house and down to Peppi's van. I took a crowbar, a bucket of sand, a torch and some bolt cutters with me.

There was no one around when I reached the van. I sprang the door open with the crowbar and shone my torch around inside. I had never seen so many tubs of ice-cream before. There was every flavour you could think of: there was apple and banana, cherry and mango, blackberry and watermelon and about fifty other flavours. Right at the end of the van were four bins with locks on them. I went over and had a look. It was just as I thought – these were his special flavours. Each one had writing on the top. This is what they said:

HAPPY ICE-CREAM for cheering people up.

NOSE ICE-CREAM for long noses.

PIMPLE ICE-CREAM for removing pimples.

SMART ICE-CREAM for smart alecs.

Now I knew his secret. That rat Dadian had been eating Smart Ice-Cream; that's how he got one hundred for Maths. I knew there couldn't be anyone as clever as me. I decided to fix Peppi up once and for all. I took out the bolt cutters and cut the locks off the four bins; then I put sand into every bin in the van. Except for the Smart Ice-Cream. I didn't put any sand in that.

I laughed to myself. Peppi wouldn't sell much ice-cream now. Not unless he started a new flavour – Sand Ice-Cream. I looked at the Smart Ice-Cream. I decided to eat some; it couldn't do any harm. Not that I needed it – I was already about as smart as you could get. Anyway, I gave it a try. I ate the lot. Once I started I couldn't stop. It tasted good. It was delicious.

I left the van and went home to bed, but I couldn't sleep. To tell the truth, I didn't feel too good. So I decided to write this. Then if any funny business has been going on you people will know what happened. I think I have made a mistake. I don't think Dadian did get any Smart Ice-Cream.

It iz the nekst day now. Somefing iz hapening to me. I don't feal quite az smart. I have bean trying to do a reel hard sum. It iz wun and wun. Wot duz wun and wun make? Iz it free or iz it for?

# Just a Guess
## Dick King-Smith

The first thing you noticed about Joe was the colour of his eyes. The table where Philip sat was close to Miss Atkinson's desk, and that morning she brought Joe into the classroom with her and stood him by her while she sat down and got out her register. All the children, boys and girls alike, were staring at the newcomer, some directly, some in a sideways fashion. There were some grins, a giggle or two. Joe looked around the room, and his eyes, Philip noticed, were a brilliant green. Cat's eyes. The bell rang.

'Good morning, children,' said Miss Atkinson.

'Good morning, Miss Atkinson. Good morning all.'

'Answer your names, please.'

Reading the register took long enough for everyone to have a good look at Joe. He was tallish, thinnish, and his clothes were not very smart. His face was very brown, his hair dark, long, a bit greasy. He did not seem embarrassed.

'Now, children,' said Miss Atkinson, 'as you can see, Top Class has grown by one this morning. This is Joe Sharp. His family has just come to stay . . . that is, to live . . . in the village. Quite a large family too, I believe. You're the youngest, aren't you, Joe?'

'Yes, Miss.'

'And how many brothers and sisters have you?'

'No sisters, Miss. Just six brothers.'

'A seventh son, are you?' said Miss Atkinson, looking up.

I wonder, she thought, is it possible, could he be the seventh son of a . . .

'Yes, Miss,' said Joe. 'My father is too.'

'Oh,' said Miss Atkinson. 'Yes. Well, now then, let me see.'

She looked round the class. 'Philip. Philip Edwards. You're a sensible person. I want you to look after Joe if you will, please. Everything will be strange for him at first. Show him where everything lives. All right?'

'Yes, Miss Atkinson,' Philip said. He saw the green eyes looking at him, and suddenly, for an instant, they shut, both together, in a kind of double wink.

'Now, Joe,' said Miss Atkinson. 'You sit next to Philip, there's room for you there, and I'll get you some exercise books. The rest of you, look at the blackboard please, and get on with the work I've put up there. Later on this morning we have an interesting visitor coming in to school to talk to you – I'll tell you . . . no, I don't think I will. We'll leave it as a surprise.'

She got up and went to the big stock cupboard at the far side of the room.

'Interesting visitor!' whispered Philip across the table.

'Hope it's Gary Lineker!'

'John Barnes,' whispered a boy opposite. 'Gary Lineker is rubbish!'

'Football!' sneered a girl, wrinkling her nose.

'Copper,' said Joe very quietly.

'What?'

'It'll be a copper.'

'How do *you* know?'

'Just a guess.'

'Shhh.'

Miss Atkinson came back with a handful of books, a pencil, a ruler, a rubber.

When the bell went for morning play-time Philip said to the new boy 'Come on then. You'd better come with me. Better put your coat on, it's cold.'

'I haven't got one,' said Joe.

'Oh,' said Philip. He put on his new anorak, blue with a red stripe down each arm and a furry hood. He felt a little awkward. 'Birthday present,' he said.

'November the twenty-third,' said Joe.

'What?' said Philip in amazement.

'Just a guess.'

'How . . . oh, I get it,' said Philip. 'You looked at the register. While Miss Atkinson was talking. You must have sharp eyes.'

'Yes,' said Joe.

In the roaring, screaming, galloping playground the two boys stood in a sheltered corner. Philip didn't feel he could dash off to play Bulldog with his particular friends, and the December winds were cold for someone without a top coat, specially somebody as thin as this one. He took a Penguin out of his anorak pocket.

'Have a bit?' he said.

'No thanks,' said Joe. 'Don't want to spoil my appetite for lunch. It's my favourite.'

'What is?'

'Spam fritters and chips.'

Clever Dick, thought Philip, I've got him this time. He hasn't seen the list in the hall. He's just a know-all. It's roast beef.

'Want to bet?' he said.

'I haven't any money,' Joe said.

'Well, I'll tell you what,' Philip said. He put his hand in his trouser pocket. 'I've got this 10p piece, see? If it is Spam fritters and chips for lunch, I'll give it to you, just give it to you. If you're wrong, well, you needn't give me anything.' That's fair, he thought. After all I do actually *know* it's roast beef.

'All right,' said Joe. The green eyes looked straight into Philip's and then shut suddenly, momentarily, in that curious double wink. Philip wanted to smile back, but he felt embarrassed and began to flip the 10p piece in the air, using the pressure of thumb against forefinger, the proper way, the way referees did. He had only lately learned to do this and was proud of it.

Joe stood by him silently, shivering a little in the cold wind. A gang of younger boys dashed past, and one shouted 'Who's your friend then, Phil?' A group of small girls in woolly hats cantered by, driving each other in harnesses made of skipping ropes. The horses neighed and the drivers cried 'Gee up!' and 'Steady!'

'Heads,' said Joe suddenly. Philip, who had been catching the coin on the back of his left hand and covering it with the fingers of his right, exposed the result of the latest toss. It was a head.

'Try again,' Philip said. He tossed the coin three times and each time Joe called correctly.

'You couldn't get it right ten times running,' said Philip, 'I bet you couldn't. Want to bet?'

'I haven't got any money,' Joe said.

'Oh, it doesn't matter. Just try it.'

Philip tossed his 10p piece ten times. Each time Joe called correctly. Philip scratched his head.

'How d'you do that?' he said.

'Just a guess.'

'You're just lucky, I reckon. Let's try it again.'

'No time,' Joe said. 'It's twenty to eleven. The bell will go any second.'

Philip looked at Joe's thin, bare wrists.

'How do you know?' he said. 'You haven't got a watch.'

The bell rang.

As they joined the rush back into school, Philip remembered what Miss Atkinson had said about an interesting visitor. What had Joe said? 'Copper.' I shouldn't be surprised, Philip found himself thinking, and then a funny shiver ran down his spine as they entered the classroom. The curtains were drawn, a screen was set up against one wall, and cables snaked across the floor to a film projector on Miss Atkinson's desk. She stood behind it, and beside her was the uniformed figure of a tall police sergeant.

'Sit down quietly, children,' said Miss Atkinson. Philip forced himself not to look at his neighbour. He didn't want to see that double wink. His mind felt swimmy. Dimly he heard snatches of talk . . . 'Sergeant Harrison . . . Road Safety Division . . . film to show you . . . ', and then a deep voice asking questions . . . 'How . . . When . . . What would you do . . . '

Hands were shooting up everywhere, and once he was conscious of Joe's voice answering something.

'Good. Very good indeed,' said the sergeant. 'I didn't expect anyone to know that one. How did you know, son?'

'Just a guess.'

Then the projector began to run. It was a good film, an interesting film designed to catch and hold children's attention, and gradually Philip began to concentrate on it. It ended with a simulated road accident, where a boy dashed suddenly across a road, right under the wheels of a double-decker bus. It was very realistic.

The projector fell silent, and the only noise in the classroom was a thin metallic ssswish as Miss Atkinson opened the curtains. The sun had come out, and the audience blinked at the sudden light.

'One last thing,' said Sergeant Harrison in his deep voice.

'One last piece of advice I've got for you lot. You've proved to me this morning that you know quite a bit about the Green Cross Code. You've answered most of my questions pretty well. I shouldn't have expected any local lad to have been able to answer that particular one.'

'Joe's new, Sergeant,' said Miss Atkinson.'It's his first day. His people are travellers – you may have seen their caravans on the common. I expect he's been all over the place, have you Joe?'

'Yes, Miss.'

'Ah, gypsy are you?' said Sergeant Harrison, but he did not say it unkindly, and he smiled as he said it.

'Yes, Sir.'

'Reckon you'll be here long?'

'No, Sir.'

Philip felt a sudden ache.

'Anyway,' said the sergeant. 'As I was saying. Here's one last piece of advice. You all saw how that film finished. Well, don't . . . think . . . it . . . can't . . . happen . . . to . . . you. We all know that was only a mock-up. The boy acting the part didn't get killed, of course. But boys do, and girls, somewhere, every day of every week of every year. So don't think "that couldn't be me". It could. So take care.'

'Paint monitors,' said Miss Atkinson a quarter of an hour later, when the screen and projector had been stowed away, and the tall sergeant had put on his peaked cap and gone. 'Angela. Sue. Judith. Would you please put the tables ready after you've had your lunch. That film should have left us all with lots of pictures in our minds. This afternoon we'll see if we can put them on paper. Now go and wash your hands, everybody, and line up by the hall door.'

Standing beside Joe in the queue, Philip listened to the pair in front.

'What is it today?'

'Roast beef.'

'Ugh!'

'Don't you like it?'

'Not much.'

They all trooped in, and when places had been settled and grace said, Mrs Wood the cook appeared in the doorway of the kitchen.

'I'm sorry, children,' she said, 'there's been a bit of a mix-up. The beef for today's lunch didn't turn up, but I don't think you'll be too disappointed.' She paused.

Philip put his hand in his pocket.

'It's Spam fritters and chips,' she said.

There were one or two 'Oh's', a loud murmur of 'MMM!s'.

'Quiet, please,' said the teacher on dinner duty.

'Keep it,' whispered Joe. 'You keep it.' Philip took his hand out of his pocket. He looked at Joe and got the double wink.

After lunch, in the playground, everybody knew. Top Class had told the rest, and somehow everyone except the littlest ones managed to pass close to the spot where Philip and Joe were standing. A gypsy! There was giggling. Philip could hear some of the passing comments and they were not kind. 'My dad says they're dirty.' 'They nick things.' 'Horses.' 'Babies.' More giggles. 'They eat hedgehogs.' A snort of laughter

'Can you tell fortunes, diddakoi?' said Mickey Bean, a big boy who was always looking for trouble and finding it. He stood in front of Joe, quite close, picking his nose with his thumb. Philip felt himself grow suddenly, furiously, angry.

'I can, Mickey,' he said in a choky voice, 'and yours is, you'll get your face smashed in.'

Mickey Bean took his thumb out and clenched his fist.

'Why, you . . .' he began, but Joe said quietly, 'Pack it in.' He looked at Mickey with his green eyes, and after a moment Mickey looked away.

'Come on, Phil,' said Joe, and they walked off together.

'That was nice of you,' he said, 'sticking up for me.'

They stood side by side at the far end of the playground, their fingers hooked through the wire mesh of the boundary fence, and stared at the traffic going up and down the village street. Philip swallowed.

'Can you?' he said. 'Tell fortunes, I mean?'

'Fortunes?' Joe said. 'I dunno about fortunes. I know what's going to happen. Sometimes. Not always, of course.'

'Well, could you . . . ' Philip looked around, ' . . . could you . . . tell what will be the next thing to come round the corner, down there, at the end of the street?'

'Probably,' Joe said. 'Want to bet?' he said, and he gave the double wink, very quickly. The twinkling of an eye, two eyes rather, thought Philip, grinning.

'I haven't got any money,' he said. 'What's in my pocket is yours, really.'

'Well, all right then, if I'm wrong,' said Joe, 'it's yours again.'

'OK,' Philip said. They stared down the street, empty for a moment.

'Private car,' Joe said. ' "S" registration. Four-door. Pale blue. Lady driving.' He paused. 'It's a Ford.'

They waited five, ten seconds. Suddenly a car came round the wall of the end house in the street, and drove up towards them, and passed them. It was a four-door 'S' registration saloon with a lady at the wheel. It was pale blue.

'It's a Vauxhall,' Philip said slowly. He looked sideways at Joe.

'Just a guess,' Joe said. 'You have a go,' he said.

Philip tried 'Red car' and got a bicycle, 'Lorry' and got the post van, 'Bus' and round the corner came an old Morris 1000. 'It's Miss Atkinson,' he said as it drew near and began to indicate to turn in to the school road. 'I expect she's been down to Beezer's, she often does at lunch time.' Beezer's was the village shop which sold everything you could imagine, and Philip was about to explain this to the new boy when it occurred to him that he needn't bother. Joe probably knew exactly what she'd bought. Before he could voice the thought, Joe said, 'All right, if you really want to know – a small brown loaf, six oranges, and a packet of Daz. Oh, and something wrapped in newspaper. Not sure what it is. It's dirty, I think.'

And of course when Miss Atkinson had disappeared into the school, and they wandered down and peeped in the car, there they were on the back seat, bread, fruit, soap-powder, and a head of celery.

Philip's earlier feeling about Joe, a scary feeling that the green eyes could somehow see into the future, had already altered quite a bit. It wasn't a feeling now, it was a certainty, and therefore not as frightening, though just as exciting.

'I suppose you know what I'm going to paint this afternoon,' he said.

'Yes,' Joe said.

At that moment the bell rang for afternoon school. The tables were ready, covered with old newspapers, the paints, brushes, palettes and mixing dishes put out.

'Painting aprons, everybody, and sleeves rolled tightly, please,' said Miss Atkinson. 'Joe Sharp, I've got an old shirt for you from my odds-and-ends cupboard.'

I know exactly what I'm going to paint, thought Philip. How curious that someone else does too. Before I've even made a mark on the paper.

He began to draw with a pencil, little figures, lots of them, like matchstick men. It was to be a picture of the children coming out of school and crossing the road. With Mrs Maybury the lollipop lady. And lots of cars and buses and lorries and motorbikes. He was so absorbed that it was some time before he realized that Joe's paper was still quite blank.

'What's the matter, Joe?' said Miss Atkinson, coming round. 'Aren't you feeling well?'

'Too many Spam fritters,' someone said, and there was giggling.

'I'm all right, Miss,' Joe said softly.

'Well, come along then. You must make a start. Think about this morning's film. Haven't you got some sort of picture in your mind?'

'Yes, Miss,' Joe said. He picked up a brush and began to put paint on his piece of paper, big splashes of it, with big brush strokes, very quickly. Miss Atkinson went away, and Philip began to colour in his matchstick men, carefully, neatly. He forgot about Joe or indeed anybody else in the room until he heard Miss Atkinson's voice again.

'Why, Joe,' she said, 'that's a strange picture. What's it supposed to be?'

'It's an accident, Miss,' Joe said, and Philip, turning to look, found the green eyes fixed on him with the strangest expression. Quickly Philip looked at Joe's picture. There were no figures in it, no shapes. There were just splodges of colour on a background of bluey-black. At one side there was something that might have been a tree, or a post perhaps, with a stripy trunk bent over in the middle, and orange blob on the end of it. Under that there was a red squidge, and in the middle of the painting a kind of chequered path with a big dark mass on it.

'Yes,' Miss Atkinson said. 'I see.'

'What is it?' Philip whispered when she had gone away. 'What's the matter? Why are you looking at me like that?'

'It's nothing,' Joe said, and then suddenly, violently, he jumped to his feet, knocking over his chair, and picking up his painting he tore it noisily across, in half, then into quarters, and then again and again till there wasn't a piece bigger than a postage stamp. Everyone stared open-mouthed.

'Joe!' cried Miss Atkinson. 'What in the world . . . ? Look, young man, I don't give out good quality paper and expensive paints so that you can . . . ' She stopped, seeing the curious pallor in the brown face. 'Are you quite sure you're feeling all right?'

'Yes, Miss. Sorry, Miss,' Joe said.

'Well, it's too late to start again now,' Miss Atkinson said. 'Put all those scraps into the wastepaper basket. The rest of you, finish off as soon as you can and start tidying up.'

'Wait for me,' Joe said, when they had been dismissed and were crossing the road with a crowd of others under

Mrs Maybury's eagle eye. It was raining and misty and getting dark all at once, and the water ran off the lollipop lady's cap and yellow oilskins. There was only one pavement in this part of the street, so everybody crossed before turning their separate ways.

'We can walk down together,' Philip said. 'If your, um, caravan's on the common, I live down that way. Our house is called . . .' 'I know,' said Joe. 'Of course,' Philip said.

'The only difference is,' he went on, 'that you can stay on this side now, but I cross over the zebra.'

'Between Beezer's and the Post Office,' Joe said.

'Yes.'

'You *mustn't*.'

'What?'

'You mustn't. Whatever you do, you mustn't go on that zebra crossing tonight.'

'Oh, but look,' Philip said, 'I promised Mum I'd always use the crossing. The traffic whizzes along here. And you heard what the policeman said this morning about zebras.'

'You mustn't,' Joe said doggedly, the rain running down his hair and making it look longer and greasier than ever.

'It was that painting of yours, wasn't it?' said Philip. 'You sort of saw something in it, did you?'

Joe nodded.

'Yes, but after all that's just . . . '

'Just a guess,' Joe said.

Philip stopped and looked into the green eyes. They shut, quickly, in the double wink, and Philip grinned.

'Oh, all right,' he said, 'if it makes you any happier I'll cross over earlier.'

They walked on a bit till they came opposite the Post Office, where there was a pavement on each side of the street. Philip looked left, looked right, looked left again, and went carefully over.

They walked on, on opposite sides now, till they came to the zebra crossing, where they stopped and faced one another across the road. It was nearly dark, and the street lights made yellow reflections in the pools of water glistening on the road.

'G'night then, Joe,' Philip called, 'See you in the morning,' but any answer was drowned in a sudden squealing of brakes. The red sports car, travelling fast, tried too suddenly to stop at the sight of two boys, both apparently about to cross. The tyres found no grip on the wet surface and the car skidded wildly sideways, straight at Joe.

Philip heard a crash, as it hit the Belisha beacon, which broke, almost in the middle, so that the top part with its orange ball came slowly down like a flag lowered to half mast.

'He guessed wrong! He guessed wrong! He guessed wrong!' went racing through Philip's brain. He had not seen Joe's wild leap to safety. The car obscured it, and the rain, and the gloom.

'Joe! Joe!' Philip shouted, and he ran madly across the zebra crossing.

He did not see the lorry, and the lorry did not see him. Until the last moment.

Which was too late.

# An Alien Stole My Brain
## Maggie Powell

Life was hard. You know what I mean. Bullies at school laughing at your clothes, stealing your pocket money, duffing up your friends. Teachers hounding you for homework, handing out punishment exercises. And nobody fancies you, especially not Laura Parker. Just when it couldn't get worse, an alien moved into my brain. No 'Please' or 'Thank you' or 'Sorry to bother you'. All I heard was,

**'Get up, lazy lump!'**

'In-a-minute.'

**'Get up now!'**

'Aaaww, you didn't have to . . .'

I opened my eyes. No Mum.

'Must be dreaming.' I lay down again.

**'We must exit now.'**

'What do you mean "we"?'

I jumped up and looked round the room. Heaps of clothes, stacks of CDs, piles of plates, usual stuff. Nobody else. Then the voice came again. From inside my head!

**'Greetings from Electra life-form to human. Short stay in brain. Nothing to worry about, there's plenty of empty space in here. I will do no harm.'**

'Huh, empty space! And what do you call this headache?'

**'Apologies. Just trying to wake you up. Stimulated the pain centre.'**

'Well, I'm awake now. Switch it off!'

I began to think of golden sand, blue sea, birds twittering and all that stuff. Weird, but at least the headache went. I got up and ready. Breakfast, bus money, packed lunch and out.

'It's freezing out here, so why am I still thinking about sunny beaches and things?'

**'Have activated "happy" mode to get you out quickly.'**

'So you've not only moved in, you've taken over! Who are you anyway? And don't try to stop me getting angry,' I added as twittering birds began to drown out my thoughts. The twittering stopped.

'And you got me out of the house with the wrong jumper, odd socks and my dopy sister's disgusting jam sandwiches . . .'

**'Run now. You are in danger of missing the bus!'**

'So, I'll get the next one.'

**'But I calculate you will be late for school.'**

'So?'

I felt my leg muscles bunch up as my hands gripped my bag. My body leaned forward, and I was off down the road like rocket-fired roller blades.

'Stop it! Nobody runs for the bus! This is embarrassing . . . . Help, I can't run this fast!' was all I could manage before my lungs went into overdrive. I jumped on the bus and ran all the way to the back seat.

'Hey, you forgot your fare,' yelled the driver.

By now I was squashed up against the Primary kids in the back seat, and still running on the spot.

**'Apologies for delay in switching off. Your wiring is faulty. Just pretend you're jogging.'**

At last I collapsed onto a seat, doing a wobbly jelly imitation. The driver was still shouting for his fare. The back seat kids sat still as statues, statues with their mouths open.

'So sorry,' I gasped. 'Go a bit . . . carried away . . . with my exercises. Could you pay . . . my fare?'

The nearest kid grabbed the money and ran to the front of the bus. He paid the fare, but didn't bother coming back up again. The stitch in my side was almost bearable as we got near the school stop.

'It's okay, I'm getting up. I don't have to run.'

The goldfish kids nodded in agreement.

'Am I thinking out loud?'

They nodded again as I got off.

I was just about to ask why it was so important to get to school on time, who he was, and what was he doing in my brain. Then I spotted Laura and pals leaning against the gate.

'Please don't make me do anything stupid. Just let me get past them quickly.'

**'No communication?'**

'Don't be stupid.'

**'But they are aware of your interest.'**

'What! How do they know that?'

**'They see your red face, goggle eyes, gulping . . . '**

'Just let me get past them.'

I was nearly in the clear when I felt my head turning back round to face Laura and my mouth stretching into a wide grin. Laura giggled, the pals sniggered.

'I'm going to kill you! I'm going to get you out of my head and mash you into mutant mince . . . But not right now. Right now I'm going to get out of Mr McLean's sight before I have to explain why I'm at school dressed like a dork.'

**'I cannot locate Mr McLean, please turn till I see.'**

'No, not a good idea, you don't stay around to be noticed!'

As I walked away I felt the head-turning thing again. But it wasn't going to happen. This time I was ready. I had a plan. Work this out, megabrain!

'Six times three is five,

Two times one is an apple,

Twelve green triangles make a horse . . .'

**'This does not compute, you are talking nonsense.'**

But at least my neck relaxed, and my head stopped turning long enough to make my escape. I went along the corridor towards the library. Not one of my usual places, but this was not one of my usual days. At least I would be able to look up books on alien possession, or even on nervous breakdowns in teenagers.

**'*You are not having a nervous breakdown.*'**

'Will you stop reading my thoughts!'

**'*There is not a lot else to do in here. This must be one of the emptiest brains on the planet.*'**

'I'll fill it up when I'm ready, with things I want to know.'

**'*Like Playstation physics and Sega science?*'**

'Like car mechanics and sport and travel . . . so if you don't like the company, you can leave. Goodbye.'

Silence.

'You still there?'

**'*Unable to leave until we get to an internet site, so that I can log on to the homing signal.*'**

That explained why we were heading to the library. It did not explain who, why, and why me.

'If you've got a homing device that means . . . this must have happened before . . . and there must be more of you. So how come I've never heard of brain invasion before?'

**'*You have. You call them dreams. Not the boring ones, but the mega adventures.*'**

'You steal our dreams?'

**'*We are your dreams. Like a game. We don't have bodies like yours, but some of your dream waves match up with our energy pulses.*'**

'My brain is an alien Playstation?'

**'*Correct. Only I left it too late to exit. But if I log out in time, no-one will have noticed.*'**

'You mean you got it wrong. Great! An alien steals my brain, and it has to be the stupidest alien in the galaxy. Why couldn't I get someone useful like the Predator!'

A shadow fell across the corridor from one of the doorways. The shadow grew into Darren, Stevie and Greg.

'Talking to yourself?' snarled Darren.

'Cos nobody else will' sneered Stevie. Greg just growled. Yes, the Predator would have been very handy just then.

'Any ideas, megabrain?' I asked. 'Any clever alien tricks?'

**'Choices for survival are fight or flight.'**

'Or give in and beg.'

**'Calculate that would make things worse.'**

The gang came nearer.

'What are my chances of flight?'

**'Distance to safe place times your performance this morning. I calculate no chance. Suggest you make noise to get attention.'**

'Like everyone will come running to save me!'

The gang was so close now, I could count the gooey green spots on Greg's neck.

**'Suggest you identify weaknesses.'**

'Can't fight, too late to run, scared as . . .'

**'Not yours! Their weaknesses!'**

'Bad breath, no style, no sense of humour . . . Hey, have you done something to my fear control?'

**'Just trying to help.'**

'If you really want to help, then turn me into a blood-sucking, thug-eating monster!'

**'Okay.'**

Power pumped through my whole body. My muscles tingled from head to toe. I threw down my bag and started to growl,

'Hwraa . . . Hwraa . . . Hwraaaaaa.'

The hairs on my arms stood on end. I licked my lips as I stared at their bare necks, watching the throb of their blood. I could smell it, sharp and salty. I wanted to taste it. I threw back my head and howled.

'He's gone mad,' sniggered Stevie. 'Let's get him.'

We ran forward at the same time, crashing into each other. I went for his neck as he tried to get his balance. My hands ripped at his shirt. My teeth bit into warm salty flesh. Somebody was screaming as we fell to the ground. I ignored the pain of the fall, too busy trying to get a grip on his neck. As I held him down, two heavy feet thudded into my back and legs. I leapt up, hands clawing, nails trying to draw blood from their horrified faces. They backed away. Stevie was whimpering on the ground. I needed blood. I snarled again and jumped at him. He kicked out, catching me on the hip. As I rolled over, Greg and Darren grabbed and pulled him away.

'Come back!' I yelled.

*'Calm it, they've gone.'*

I wiped my wet mouth as my body tingled back to normal. There was blood on my hand.

'I'll need to wash this cut.'

*'It's not your blood.'*

I felt the saliva drain from my mouth, and my stomach turn over.

'Whose blood?' I whispered. 'Stevie's?'

*'You asked me to turn you into a blood-sucking, thug-eating . . . '*

'Okay, okay . . . I didn't think you could. Now they'll tell everyone. What will Laura think?'

*'I calculate they'll tell no-one, but will keep out of your way.'*

'Thanks, but that was disgusting.'

*'Imagine some of that chewing gum, to take away the taste.'*

'Oh, it's all very well for you.'

*'No, it wasn't. I was right in there with you. Supposing you had gone for Greg. Imaging chewing all those squishy spots.'*

'I am going to be SICK!'

*'Here, try these nice tastes.'*

I was too tired to stop the flow of peppermint, vanilla ice cream, chocolate mousse, banana chews, Kola cubes. Some of these tastes were from playschool!

'Stop raiding my memory, there's some private stuff in there.'

By now we were at the library. Laura was doing her homework. No sign of the pals. She smiled. Before I could stop it, I smiled back.

**'That wasn't me. You did that yourself.'**

'I know, I know. Let's get you downloaded. I've got a life to lead.'

The voice helped me to key into the internet and select the website. Rows of words and numbers flashed onto the screen. Too fast to read. Too fast for any human to read. Then a twisty spiral spun in the centre of the screen.

**'We have contact. All you have to do is keep your hand on the control, and relax your mind, and slowly, slowly, deep, deep, sleepy, sleep . . .'**

'Will I see you again?' I yawned.

**'Hope not.'**

'Me too.'

The voice faded. I yawned again as I watched the screen. A face began to grow in the centre of the spiral, a face with long hair, wide eyes and a smile like Laura's. Then it all went blank.

I stared open-mouthed at the empty screen. I couldn't believe it! An alien stole my brain . . . and it was a GIRL!!!!

# Riding the Silver Wave
## Ben Bo

Midnight, and Craig was at the window again. He was standing in the shadows, just staring out at the ocean.

'He scares me, Dad,' I whispered. 'He's there every night.'

I had shaken our dad half awake and told him to come quick. Now he stood at the door, his face all crumpled up with sleep. 'What's the daft beggar doing?' he growled.

'He's asleep,' I said. 'It's always the same. He sees something out there – something bad.'

Craig sucked in his breath. His blank eyes fixed on the waves somewhere just off the beach, near the jagged rocks of Cove Bay Point.

I crept over to stand beside him and looked out. The moon was big and fat, almost full. Below our shack, beyond the dunes and the bushes of Three-cornered Jacks, I could see the beach. The sand gleamed like silver. The sea was spread wide and black. The waves were rolling in like always, only now their crests were foaming with moonlight.

'Look out!' Craig shouted and made me jump. 'He'll never make it – no way.'

'Who is it, Craig?' I asked. 'Who can you see?'

'He's got to cut back! Cut back!' Craig said. He was sweating now. 'He's taking the drop. It's suicide. He'll wipe out in the tube!' His eyes flicked, dancing from wave to wave. He gripped the windowsill, knuckles bone-white. 'Watch out for the rocks! The rocks! Noooooooooooooooooooo!' He staggered back.

'It's OK!' I said.

Craig seemed to feel my touch on his arm. He turned, but I could tell he couldn't see me. His stare just went right through, as if I wasn't there. Then he just shuffled away and got back into bed.

'Why does he do that, Dad?' I asked.

Dad scratched the stubble on his chin. 'I reckon the sun's got to him, Josh,' he said.

But as I lay in bed and stared up at the ceiling, I decided it was true what the others said. They said Craig had lost it. They said he was scared, and he had been like that ever since Johnny-boy had died.

I felt the pull of the wave long before it reached me. I had counted in six already. They were coming in sets of seven, and I knew the seventh would be the biggest. Craig had taught me that.

In front of me, I could see the beach. To my left, the jagged rocks of Cove Bay Point. Behind, the sparkling blue wave I was going to ride.

This was the big one and I was all knotted up inside. Craig had warned me about the power of a big wave. How it could look good but curl in early and smash you onto the rocks. How it could suck you down and take you far out to sea – just like the one which had taken Johnny-boy.

They had been mates, him and Craig. The best surfers in Cove Bay, everyone said. But when I asked Craig about it, he just looked away. He said Johnny-boy was crazy, and told me not to listen to what the other surfies said.

But I had heard the talk in Happy Larry's Café. I had heard the rumours about the Silver Wave. The wave that came at night and only on the full moon tide. It was a ghost wave, they said, and only a fool or the devil would dare to take the drop on it.

But that hadn't stopped Johnny-boy. He had gone out to ride it alone. He wanted to prove he was the best and that he wasn't scared of anything. They never did find his body.

I shivered even though the Aussie sun was hot on my back as I lay floating on my surfboard. But I couldn't back out now. Ratso and his mates were watching me.

They said I wouldn't do it as they watched me stripe my face blue and yellow with zinc sun block – war paint we called it – they said I was chicken, like Craig. But I was about to prove them all wrong.

The seventh wave came in with a rush. I could feel the power of it sucking at the long, leaf-shaped board beneath me. I watched the water rise up behind me into a sparkling mountain of blues and greens, and the foam on the top looked like snow.

I paddled forward with both hands, then the wave scooped me up. It pushed me forward, faster and faster. I gripped the sides of my board and jumped up, tucking my legs in quickly. My feet slapped on the flat of the board. And I was standing – wobbling a lot, maybe, but standing all the same – riding the wave like a sea spirit.

Then, suddenly, the wave just swallowed me up like a giant mouth. It sucked me down and rolled me around its bubbling green tongue. I tumbled round and round, then it spat me out as if I didn't taste good. I hit the bottom and felt all the air bubble out of me. My nose and mouth filled with salty water. After that, I was just rolling, rolling, rolling, until I thought I would never stop.

I crawled out and spat what felt like an ocean onto the sand. 'What a wipe out!' I gasped, glad that my surfboard was still attached to my ankle by its plastic leash.

Craig had seen what had happened. 'You crazy idiot!' he said. 'You're not good enough for a wave that big.'

I could see Ratso and the others laughing and pointing.

'Leave it out, Craig!' I said. 'Just 'cos you're too scared to go out any more doesn't mean I can't!' I didn't mean to say it, it just sort of came out. I could see I'd hurt him.

'You think you know everything, don't you, Josh?' he said. 'But you don't!'

I had heard it all before, so I picked up my surfboard and stomped off.

'And stay away from Ratso, he's bad news!' I heard him call after me.

Now he was even telling me who my friends should be.

'Is Craigie playing nursie to his baby brother again?' Ratso jeered as I passed. The others thought that was dead funny.

'Shut it, Ratso!' I hissed.

'You gonna make me?' he said, then smiled and he shook his head. 'Na! I forgot you're chicken like your brother!'

'You take that back!'

Ratso's mates surrounded me. Five against one. It didn't look good. I had to think fast.

'Crack-a-can!' I said.

Ratso grinned. 'Are you challenging *me*?'

I nodded. 'Crack-a-can. Half an hour. Happy Larry's Café,' I said. 'Then we'll see who's chicken.'

Ratso's mates danced about with excitement.

'You'll be sorry!' Ratso said and laughed.

'He's always saying stuff like that about us,' I told Craig, as I stashed my board back at the shack.

Craig sat on the steps and looked out at the sea. 'Who cares what he thinks?' he said. 'Just let it go.'

That made me mad. 'What's happened to you, Craig? You used to be so cool. You used to be the best. Now you're – ' I couldn't say it. I couldn't put in words the disappointment I felt inside.

I pulled on an old T-shirt and my jeans, and grabbed my bike. Whatever Craig was – or wasn't – it didn't make me the same, I had decided. I would prove I wasn't scared of anything, and I would do it as many times as I needed to. That was why I rode down to Happy Larry's Café that day. That was why I promised to ride the Silver Wave.

I took the short cut down Seagull Avenue and left my bike by the door. Happy Larry's Café was fuller than usual by the time I arrived. Word about my challenge had got around.

'What's going on?' Happy Larry growled, polishing the top of his counter with a dirty rag. He didn't look happy at all.

Ratso was waiting, sitting at the table in the corner.

'Who's going to be ref?' I asked, sitting down opposite him.

'Danny,' he said, nodding towards a girl with dark hair. I nodded. Danny was OK.

Danny put the six cans of Coke on the table and the crowd went quiet. She chose one and held it up so everyone could see. Then she started shaking it. She shook and shook, until we all knew it would explode like a bomb if it was opened. Then she put it back on the table and started switching the cans around. She muddled them all up good and proper, until no-one knew which one was which.

'You know the rules,' Ratso said. 'Whoever gets the bomb has to skull all of them, then we – '

'I know what happens then,' I said, trying to sound as tough as one of those poker players I had seen in old Westerns.

'Six to one chance!' Danny said to the crowd.

Ratso chose first. He picked a can held it in front of his face and pulled the ring on the top. *Crack! Pfsst!*

He grinned. 'Now let's see if you're as chicken as your brother.'

'Five to one,' Danny called out the odds.

I didn't hesitate, just reached out and chose. I lifted the can to my face. *Crack! Pfsst!*

Everyone relaxed, murmuring and shuffling their feet.

The smile faded from Ratso's face. The odds were getting worse. He had a one in four chance of picking the bomb. His hand hovered over one can for a moment, then he chose another. *Crack! Pfsst!* He blew out a sigh and grinned.

'I'm no chicken,' I said as Danny called the odds out at three to one. I picked a can and held it to my face, but before I cracked it I said, 'And I'll prove it by riding the Silver Wave.' Then I closed my eyes. *Crack! Pfsst!*

You could have heard a moth sneeze after that. They all just stared at me, mouths open. It was Ratso who broke the silence.

"You know what happened to Johnny-boy,' he said, quietly, 'and he was the best.'

I nodded. I knew.

Ratso was sweating now. 'It comes on the full moon tide – that's tonight.'

'I said I would do it,' I snapped. 'Now you crack a can!'

Ratso just stared at me across the table, a weird look in his eyes. Then, as if in a dream, he reached out and chose one of the two remaining cans. He lifted it to his face slowly. His finger hooked into the metal ring on the top and he closed his eyes.

We waited.

'That's enough!' Happy Larry said, bursting through the crowd suddenly. He snatched the can away from Ratso.

*Crack! Pfsst!* Ratso's finger caught in the ring-pull.

'I've warned you lot about this before,' Happy Larry boomed, but he never did get the chance to throw us all out.

The can shook in his huge hand. He looked at it and frowned. Then a great gush of Coke whooshed up into the air as the bomb exploded. Up it came and kept coming, jetting out through the hole in the top. Most of it hit him smack in the face.

And suddenly we were all piling out of Happy Larry's Café and running in every direction. I jumped on my bike, but Ratso blocked my way.

'Not so fast, big mouth!' he said. 'If you are going to ride the Silver Wave you'd better be at Cove Bay Point by midnight.'

'I'll be there,' I said.

'And I'll be waiting.'

I woke suddenly. The light from the full moon was streaming into my face through a gap in the curtains. I sat up. Craig's bed was empty, the sheets crumpled and thrown back.

'Craig!' I whispered. He didn't answer.

I slipped out of bed and over to the window. Below, the sea was frothing and foaming in the moonlight. The dark waves crashed onto the beach, driven by the wind and the full moon tide. Then I saw Ratso. He was just a shadow against the silver sand, but I could see he had his surfboard tucked under his arm.

I changed into my shorts and let myself out of the shack as quietly as the squeaky door would let me. I picked up my surfboard and sprinted for the beach. The tough grass whipped my legs and the sand was icy cold under my feet as I ran.

'Thought you'd chickened out,' Ratso said, as I scrambled over the last dune.

He was standing at the water's edge, the wind whipping his hair about and his eyes glowing with that weird light again.

The sea was dark and ugly. A wave roared in and the foam rushed up around my ankles. I felt the cold, and suddenly I was scared. Dead scared.

'Maybe we should just forget all about it,' I said.

I glanced over my shoulder nervously. The dunes were lumpy with shadows. I could see our shack in the moonlight. It was dark, like the others along the beach front. Only the streetlight in Seagull Avenue shone out in the night.

'It's too late to back out now,' Ratso said. He splashed out, lay on his surfboard and began paddling with both hands. He ducked through a wave then bobbed up on the other side.

'What's going on?' a voice asked suddenly. It was Craig. He must have seen us from the shack. He came sliding down a sand dune in a shower of sand and shook me by my shoulders.

'It's Ratso,' I said. 'He's gone out to ride the Silver Wave.'

Craig's face went very pale. 'I've got to stop him,' he gasped, 'before it's too late.'

He ran into the water and plunged into a wave. I just stood there and watched, not knowing what to do. Then I lost him and I wondered if I should follow or go for help. Ratso had vanished too. I panicked. I thought they had both drowned, then suddenly the waves parted and I saw them: Craig thrashing through the water; Ratso too far out and in trouble.

I didn't think twice after that. Craig was going to need all the help he could get and I knew it. I flung myself onto my board and paddled as fast as I could, but I was only halfway out when I saw Ratso go under. A wave rolled over me and I came up just in time to see Craig pull him up again. Then another wave hit me and I lost sight of them.

I suppose I should have known. I suppose I should have realized something was very wrong when I saw the boy sitting cross-legged on his board. The waves didn't seem to touch him. He was drifting through them like they weren't even there But he had his back to me so I couldn't see him properly. It was only when I was closer that I notice how thin and skinny he was. Only then did I noticed his hair was like plaited seaweed and that his surfboard was glowing electric blue in the water.

I called out. He turned slowly. Then I saw his face, and screamed.

No eyes. No skin. No lips. Just grinning teeth and bone. A white skull face. Dead, but alive.

'You want to ride the Silver Wave with me?' the boy with the skull-face asked. He pointed a bone finger out to sea.

Then I saw it – a monster of a wave rolling towards me. It sparkled with moonlight as if it was made of diamonds. A moving mass of silver, solid yet silent. A ghost wave. And as I watched, I knew I would never escape it.

I turned back towards the shore, but it was too late. The wave reared up behind me. I paddled like crazy, my board cut through the water under me, but it caught me easily. Then suddenly I knew what I had to do.

I gripped the sides of my board and jumped up. My feet slapped on fibreglass, and I was standing. I didn't have time to think, I just did everything automatically. I shifted my weight, angling my board into the wave, and felt the wind on my face as I skimmed across the silver water.

Just for one moment, I thought I could ride the wave and beat it. Then I looked up and saw the water begin to curl in over my head. It came right over until it formed a sparkling tube – a pipe of pure silver – with me racing down the middle.

At the end, ragged, jagged rocks waited like big black teeth foaming in a sea of spit. I knew they would chew me to bits if I hit them, but I couldn't escape. I could only go faster and faster down that tube of death.

Then, all of a sudden, out of the middle of the wave came the boy with the skull face. A hole just opened up in the water and out he shot, crouching on his board. He was glowing like a neon sign, his seaweed hair flying in the wind. He grinned at me and surfed alongside for what seemed like a million years. Then he cut straight in front of me, slicing right across the point of my surfboard.

I felt a shudder as the fins on the underside of his board slashed deep into mine. After that I was going down, but before I went under I saw him surf on. He shot through the rocks as if they weren't even there and disappeared in a blinding flash of light. I saw him do it before I went under.

I struggled at first, then I just sank until I hit the bottom. A stream of bubbles blew out of my mouth and burst into a million coloured stars. The stars spun around in front of my eyes, then changed into starfish. Above, I could see the moon, and the waves racing towards the shore. I could imagine the sting of the salt and the howl of the wind. But down below, everything was quiet and calm.

I think I would have stayed there for ever if someone hadn't pulled me up. I'm sure we went up together, but I broke the surface alone. After that, I remember the waves tossing me about and being thrown onto the sand like a piece of old driftwood. Then everything went dark.

Craig let the sand trickle through his fingers and blow away in the breeze.

We were sitting on a sand dune, looking out at the rocks of Cove Bay Point. Two days had passed since they had pumped the water out of me.

'It was him, wasn't it?' I said.

He nodded without taking his eyes off the sea. The water was blue now and the rocks weren't like teeth any more.

'I have never told anyone this,' Craig said in a quiet voice, 'but it was my fault Johnny-boy died.'

My heart started thumping. 'How do you mean?'

He looked at me with sad eyes. 'I let him go out alone. I couldn't stop him. He just kept saying if he rode the Silver Wave it would prove he was the best. So I waited here on the beach. Then I saw him hit the rocks, but I couldn't help him . . . '

And suddenly it all made sense: the bad dreams, the way Craig had been acting – everything.

'It wasn't your fault,' I said. 'You can't blame yourself.'

We sat in silence for a long while after that, just watching the waves roll in. Then Craig stood up and brushed the sand off his shorts.

'Johnny-boy saved me from the rocks,' I said, pointing to the deep scratches across the point of my surfboard.

'I guess so,' he said.

'Maybe it was his way of saying *you* were right and he was wrong,' I said. 'Maybe his ghost is out there somewhere, ready to stop anyone else making the same mistake as him.'

He thought for a moment, then he did something I had not seen him do for a very long time – he smiled.

Craig won an award for saving Ratso's life, which was good because, apart from anything else, it shut Ratso up. And the bad dreams stopped after he told Dad and the others about Johnny-boy. No-one blamed him for what had happened.

Me, I learned what I should have known all along: that my brother was the best, and that sometimes it takes more guts to say *no*.

As for Johnny-boy, nobody knows if his ghost still guards those rocks on Cove Bay Point. So if you want to find out for sure – and you dare – you will just have to ride the Silver Wave yourself.

# Man from the South
## Roald Dahl

It was getting on towards six o'clock so I thought I'd buy myself a beer and go out and sit in a deck-chair by the swimming-pool and have a little evening sun.

I went to the bar and got the beer and carried it outside and wandered down the garden towards the pool.

It was a fine garden with lawns and beds of azaleas and tall coconut palms, and the wind was blowing strongly through the tops of the palm trees, making the leaves hiss and crackle as though they were on fire. I could see the clusters of big brown nuts hanging down underneath the leaves.

There were plenty of deck-chairs around the swimming-pool and there were white tables and huge brightly-coloured umbrellas and sunburned men and women sitting around in bathing suits. In the pool itself there were three or four girls and about a dozen boys, all splashing about and making a lot of noise and throwing a large rubber ball at one another.

I stood watching them. The girls were English girls from the hotel. The boys I didn't know about, but they sounded American, and I thought they were probably naval cadets who'd come ashore from the US naval training vessel which had arrived in harbour that morning.

I went over and sat down under a yellow umbrella where there were four empty seats, and I poured my beer and settled back comfortably with a cigarette.

It was very pleasant sitting there in the sunshine with beer and cigarette. It was pleasant to sit and watch the bathers splashing about in the green water.

The American sailors were getting on nicely with the English girls. They'd reached the stage where they were diving under the water and tipping them up by their legs.

Just then I noticed a small, oldish man walking briskly around the edge of the pool. He was immaculately dressed in a white suit and he walked very quickly with little bounding strides, pushing himself high up on to his toes with each step. He had on a large creamy Panama hat, and he came bouncing along the side of the pool, looking at the people and the chairs.

He stopped beside me and smiled, showing two rows of very small, uneven teeth, slightly tarnished. I smiled back.

'Excuse pleess, but may I sit here?'

'Certainly,' I said. 'Go ahead.'

He bobbed around to the back of the chair and inspected it for safety, then he sat down and crossed his legs. His white buck-skin shoes had little holes punched all over them for ventilation.

'A fine evening,' he said. 'They are all evenings fine here in Jamaica.' I couldn't tell if the accent were Italian or Spanish, but I felt fairly sure he was some sort of a South American. And old too, when you saw him close. Probably around sixty-eight or seventy.

'Yes,' I said. 'It is wonderful here, isn't it.'

'And who, might I ask, are all dese? Dese is no hotel people.' He was pointing at the bathers in the pool.

'I think they're American sailors,' I told him. 'They're Americans who are learning to be sailors.'

'Of course dey are Americans. Who else in de world is going to make as much noise as dat? You are not American, no?'

'No,' I said. 'I am not.'

Suddenly one of the American cadets was standing in front of us. He was dripping wet from the pool and one of the English girls was standing there with him.

'Are these chairs taken?' he said.

'No,' I answered.

'Mind if I sit down?'

'Go ahead.'

'Thanks,' he said. He had a towel in his hand and when he sat down he unrolled it and produced a pack of cigarettes and a lighter. He offered the cigarettes to the girl and she refused; then he offered them to me and I took one. The little man said, 'Tank you, no, but I tink I have a cigar.' He pulled out a crocodile case and got himself a cigar, then he produced a knife which had a small scissors in it and he snipped the end off the cigar.

'Here, let me give you a light.' The American boy held up his lighter.

'Dat will not work in dis wind.'

'Sure it'll work. It always works.'

The little man removed his unlighted cigar from his mouth, cocked his head on one side and looked at the boy.

'*All*-ways?' he said slowly.

'Sure, it never fails. Not with me anyway.'

The little man's head was still cocked over on one side and he was still watching the boy. 'Well, well. So you say dis famous lighter it never fails. Iss dat you say?'

'Sure,' the boy said. 'That's right.' He was about nineteen or twenty with a long freckled face and a rather sharp birdlike nose. His chest was not very sunburned and there were freckles there too, and a few wisps of pale-reddish hair. He was holding the lighter in his right hand, ready to flip the wheel. 'It never fails,' he said, smiling now because he was purposely exaggerating his little boast. 'I promise you it never fails.'

'One momint, pleess.' The hand that held the cigar came up high, palm outward, as though it were stopping traffic. 'Now juss one momint.' He had a curiously soft, toneless voice and he kept looking at the boy all the time.

'Shall we not perhaps make a little bet on dat?' He smiled at the boy. 'Shall we not make a little bet on whether your lighter lights?'

'Sure, I'll bet,' the boy said, 'Why not?'

'You like to bet?'

'Sure, I'll always bet.'

The man paused and examined his cigar, and I must say I didn't much like the way he was behaving. It seemed he was already trying to make something out of this, and to embarrass the boy, and at the same time I had the feeling he was relishing a private little secret all his own.

He looked up again at the boy and said slowly, 'I like to bet, too. Why we don't have a good bet on dis ting? A good big bet.'

'Now wait a minute,' the boy said. 'I can't do that. But I'll bet you a quarter. I'll even bet you a dollar or whatever it is over here – some shillings, I guess.'

The little man waved his hand again. 'Listen to me. Now we have some fun. We make a bet. Den we go up to my room here in de hotel where iss no wind and I bet you you cannot light dis famous lighter of yours ten times running without missing once.'

'I'll bet I can,' the boy said.

'All right. Good. We make a bet, yes?'

'Sure, I'll bet you a buck.'

'No, no. I make you a very good bet. I am rich man and I am sporting man also. Listen to me. Outside de hotel iss my car. Iss very fine car. American car from your country. Cadillac – '

'Hey now. Wait a minute.' The boy leaned back in his deck-chair and he laughed. 'I can't put up that sort of property. This is crazy.'

'Not crazy at all. You strike lighter successfully ten times running and Cadillac is yours. You like to have dis Cadillac, yes?'

'Sure, I'd like to have a Cadillac.' The boy was still grinning.

'All right. Fine. We make a bet and I put up my Cadillac.'

'And what do I put up?'

The little man carefully removed the red band from his still unlighted cigar. 'I never ask you, my friend, to bet something you cannot afford. You understand?'

'Then what do I bet?'

'I make it very easy for you, yes?'

'OK. You make it easy.'

'Some small ting you can afford to give away, and if you did happen to lose it you would not feel too bad. Right?'

'Such as what?'

'Such as, perhaps, de little finger on your left hand.'

'My *what*?' The boy stopped grinning.

'Yes. Why not? You win, you take de car. You looss, I take de finger.'

'I don't get it. How d'you mean, you take the finger?'

'I chop it off.'

'Jumping jeepers! That's a crazy bet. I think I'll just make it a dollar.'

The little man leaned back, spread out his hands palms upwards and gave a tiny contemptuous shrug of the shoulders. 'Well, well, well,' he said. 'I do not understand. You say it lights but you will not bet. Den we forget it, yes?'

The boy sat quite still, staring at the bathers in the pool. Then he remembered suddenly he hadn't lighted his cigarette. He put it between his lips, cupped his hands around the lighter and flipped the wheel. The wick lighted and burned with a small, steady, yellow flame and the way he held his hands the wind didn't get to it at all.

'Could I have a light, too?' I said.

'God, I'm sorry, I forgot you didn't have one.'

I held out my hand for the lighter, but he stood up and came over to do it for me.

'Thank you,' I said, and he returned to his seat.

'You having a good time?' I asked.

'Fine,' he answered. 'It's pretty nice here.'

There was a silence then, and I could see that the little man had succeeded in disturbing the boy with his absurd proposal. He was sitting there very still, and it was obvious that a small tension was beginning to build up inside him. Then he started shifting about in his seat, and rubbing his chest, and stroking the back of his neck, and finally he placed both hands on his knees and began tap-tapping with his fingers against the knee-caps. Soon he was tapping with one of his feet as well.

'Now just let me check up on this bet of yours,' he said at last. 'You say we go up to your room and if I make this lighter light ten times running I win a Cadillac. If it misses just once then I forfeit the little finger of my left hand. Is that right?'

'Certainly. Dat is de bet. But I tink you are afraid.'

'What do we do if I lose? Do I have to hold my finger out while you chop it off?'

'Oh, no! Dat would be no good. And you might be tempted to refuse to hold it out. What I should do I should tie one of your hands to de table before we started and I should stand dere with a knife ready to go *chop* de momint your lighter missed.'

'What year is the Cadillac?' the boy asked.

'Excuse. I not understand.'

'What year – how old is the Cadillac?'

'Ah! How old? Yes. It is last year. Quite new car. But I see you are not betting man. Americans never are.'

The boy paused for just a moment and he glanced first at the English girl, then at me. 'Yes,' he said sharply. 'I'll bet you.'

'Good!' The little man clapped his hands together quietly, once. 'Fine,' he said. 'We do it now. And you, sir,' he turned to me, 'you would perhaps be good enough to, what you call it, to – to referee.' He had pale, almost colourless eyes with tiny black pupils.

'Well,' I said. 'I think it's a crazy bet. I don't think I like it very much.'

'Nor do I,' said the English girl. It was the first time she'd spoken. 'I think it's a stupid, ridiculous bet.'

'Are you serious about cutting off this boy's finger if he loses?' I said.

'Certainly I am. Also about giving him Cadillac if he win. Come now. We go to my room.'

He stood up. 'You like to put on some clothes first?' he said.

'No,' the boy answered. 'I'll come like this.' Then he turned to me. 'I'd consider it a favour if you'd come along and referee.'

'All right,' I said. 'I'll come along, but I don't like the bet.'

'You come too,' he said to the girl. 'You come and watch.'

The little man led the way back through the garden to the hotel. He was animated now, and excited, and that seemed to make him bounce up higher than ever on his toes as he walked along.

'I live in annexe,' he said. 'You like to see car first? Iss just here.'

He took us to where we could see the front driveway of the hotel and he stopped and pointed to a sleek pale-green Cadillac parked close by.

'Dere she iss. De green one. You like?'

'Say, that's a nice car,' the boy said.

'All right. Now we go up and see if you can win her.'

We followed him into the annexe and up one flight of stairs. He unlocked his door and we all trooped into what was a large pleasant double bedroom. There was a woman's dressing-gown lying across the bottom of one of the beds.

'First,' he said, 'we 'ave a little Martini.'

The drinks were on a small table in the far corner, all ready to be mixed, and there was a shaker and ice and plenty of glasses. He began to make the Martini, but meanwhile he'd rung the bell and now there was a knock on the door and a coloured maid came in.

'Ah!' he said, putting down the bottle of gin, taking a wallet from his pocket and pulling out a pound note. 'You will do something for me now, pleess.' He gave the maid the pound.

'You keep dat,' he said. 'And now we are going to play a little game in here and I want you to go off and find for me two – no tree tings. I want some nails, I want a hammer, and I want a chopping knife, a butcher's chopping knife which you can borrow from the kitchen. You can get, yes?'

'A *chopping knife!*' The maid opened her eyes wide and clasped her hands in front of her. 'You mean a *real* chopping knife'

'Yes, yes, of course. Come on now, pleess. You can find dose tings surely for me.'

'Yes, sir, I'll try, sir. Surely I'll try to get them.' And she went.

The little man handed round the Martinis. We stood there and sipped them, the boy with the long freckled face and the pointed nose, bare-bodied except for a pair of faded brown bathing shorts; the English girl, a large-boned fair-haired girl wearing a pale blue bathing suit, who watched the boy over the top of her glass all the time; the little man with the colourless eyes standing there in his immaculate white suit drinking his Martini and looking at the girl in her pale blue bathing dress. I didn't know what to make of it all. The man seemed serious about the bet and he seemed serious about the business of cutting off the finger. But hell, what if the boy lost? Then we'd have to rush him to the hospital in the Cadillac that he hadn't won. That would be a fine thing. Now wouldn't that be a really fine thing? It would be a damn silly unnecessary thing so far as I could see.

'Don't you think this is rather a silly bet?' I said.

'I think it's a fine bet,' the boy answered. He had already downed one large Martini.

'I think it's a stupid, ridiculous bet,' the girl said. 'What'll happen if you lose?'

'It won't matter. Come to think of it, I can't remember ever in my life having had any use for the little finger on my left hand. Here he is.' The boy took hold of the finger. 'Here he is and he hasn't ever done a thing for me yet. So why shouldn't I bet him? I think it's a fine bet.'

The little man smiled and picked up the shaker and refilled our glasses.

'Before we begin,' he said, 'I will present to de – to de referee de key of de car.' He produced a car key from his pocket and gave it to me. 'De papers,' he said, 'de owning papers and insurance are in de pocket of de car.'

Then the coloured maid came in again. In one hand she carried a small chopper, the kind used by butchers for chopping meat bones, and in the other a hammer and a bag of nails.

'Good! You get dem all. Tank you, tank you. Now you can go.' He waited until the maid had closed the door, then he put the implements on one of the beds and said, 'Now we prepare ourselves, yes?' And to the boy, 'Help me, pleess, with dis table. We carry it out a little.'

It was the usual kind of hotel writing desk, just a plain rectangular table about four feet by three with a blotting pad, ink, pens and paper. They carried it out into the room away from the wall, and removed the writing things.

'And now,' he said, 'a chair.' He picked up a chair and placed it beside the table. He was very brisk and very animated, like a person organizing games at a children's party. 'And now de nails. I must put in de nails.' He fetched the nails and he began to hammer them into the top of the table.

We stood there, the boy, the girl, and I, holding Martinis in our hands, watching the little man at work.

We watched him hammer two nails into the table, about six inches apart. He didn't hammer them right home; he allowed a small part of each one to stick up. Then he tested them for firmness with his fingers.

Anyone would think the son of a bitch had done this before, I told myself. He never hesitates. Table, nails, hammer, kitchen chopper. He knows exactly what he needs and how to arrange it.

'And now,' he said, 'all we want is some string.' He found some string. 'All right, at last we are ready. Will you pleess to sit here at de table?' he said to the boy.

The boy put his glass away and sat down.

'Now place de left hand between dese two nails. De nails are only so I can tie your hand in place. All right, good. Now I tie your hand secure to de table – so.'

He wound the string around the boy's wrist, then several times around the wide part of the hand, then he fastened it tight to the nails. He made a good job of it and when he'd finished there wasn't any question about the boy being able to draw his hand away. But he could move his fingers.

'Now pleess, clench de fist, all except for de little finger. You must leave de little finger sticking out, lying on de table.'

'*Ex*-cellent! *Ex*-cellent! Now we are ready. Wid your right hand you manipulate de lighter. But one momint, pleess.'

He skipped over to the bed and picked up the chopper. He came back and stood beside the table with the chopper in his hand.

'We are all ready?' he said. 'Mister referee, you must say to begin.'

The English girl was standing there in her pale blue bathing costume right behind the boy's chair. She was just standing there, not saying anything. The boy was sitting quite still holding the lighter in his right hand, looking at the chopper. The little man was looking at me.

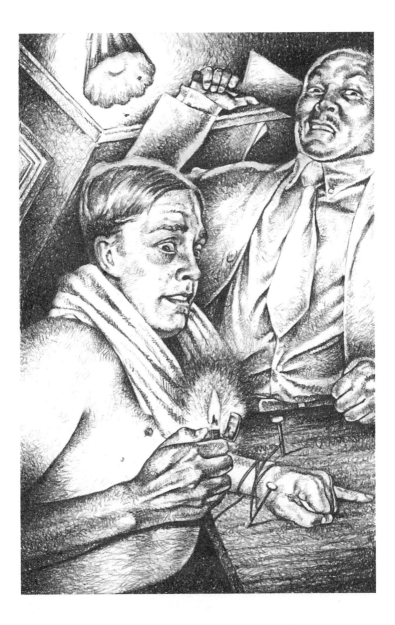

'Are you ready?' I asked the boy.

'I'm ready.'

'And you?' to the little man.

'Quite ready,' he said and he lifted the chopper up in the air and held it there about two feet above the boy's finger, ready to chop. The boy watched it, but he didn't flinch and his mouth didn't move at all. He merely raised his eyebrows and frowned.

'All right,' I said. 'Go ahead.'

The boy said, 'Will you please count aloud the number of times I light it.'

'Yes,' I said. 'I'll do that.'

With his thumb he raised the top of the lighter, and again with the thumb he gave the wheel a sharp flick. The flint sparked and the wick caught fire and burned with a small yellow flame.

'One!' I called.

He didn't blow the flame out; he closed the top of the lighter on it and he waited for perhaps five seconds before opening it again.

He flicked the wheel very strongly and once more there was a small flame burning on the wick.

'Two!'

No one else said anything. The boy kept his eyes on the lighter. The little man held the chopper up in the air and he too was watching the lighter.

'Three!'

'Four!'

'Five!'

'Six!'

'Seven!' Obviously it was one of those lighters that worked. The flint gave a big spark and the wick was the right length. I watched the thumb snapping the top down on to the flame. Then a pause. Then the thumb raising the top once more. This was an all-thumb operation. The thumb did everything. I took a breath, ready to say eight. The thumb flicked the wheel. The flint sparked. The little flame appeared.

'Eight!' I said, and as I said it the door opened. We all turned and we saw a woman standing in the doorway, a small, black-haired woman, rather old, who stood there for about two seconds then rushed forward, shouting, 'Carlos! Carlos!' She grabbed his wrist, took the chopper from him, threw it on the bed, took hold of the little man by the lapels of his white suit and began shaking him very vigorously, talking to him fast and loud and fiercely all the time in some Spanish-sounding language. She shook him so fast you couldn't see him any more. He became a faint, misty, quickly moving outline, like the spokes of a turning wheel.

Then she slowed down and the little man came into view again and she hauled him across the room and pushed him backwards on to one of the beds. He sat on the edge of it blinking his eyes and testing his head to see if it would still turn on his neck.

'I am sorry,' the woman said. 'I am so terribly sorry that this should happen.' She spoke almost perfect English.

'It is too bad,' she went on. 'I suppose it is really my fault. For ten minutes I leave him alone to go and have my hair washed and I come back and he is at it again.' She looked sorry and deeply concerned.

The boy was untying his hand from the table. The English girl and I stood there and said nothing.

'He is a menace,' the woman said. 'Down where we live at home he has taken altogether forty-seven fingers from different people, and he has lost eleven cars. In the end they threatened to have him put away somewhere. That's why I brought him up here.'

'We were only having a little bet,' mumbled the little man from the bed.

'I suppose he bet you a car,' the woman said.

'Yes,' the boy answered. 'A Cadillac.'

'He has no car. It's mine. And that makes it worse,' she said, 'that he should bet you when he has nothing to bet with. I am ashamed and very sorry about it all.' She seemed an awfully nice woman.

'Well,' I said, 'then here's the key of your car.' I put it on the table.

'We were only having a little bet,' mumbled the little man.

'He hasn't anything left to bet with,' the woman said. 'He hasn't a thing in the world. Not a thing. As a matter of fact I myself won it all from him a long while ago. It took time, a lot of time, and it was hard work, but I won it all in the end.' She looked up at the boy and she smiled, a slow sad smile, and she came over and put out a hand to take the key from the table.

I can see it now, that hand of hers; it had only one finger on it, and a thumb.

# Karate for Kids
## Terence Blacker

You're probably not going to believe this. Pretty soon you'll be saying, Oh please. Gimme a break. Pull the other one, guy.

So maybe I'd better just lay it on you straight, no messing.

My name is Kick.

Better known to my readers as *Karate for Kids*.

Better known to Miss Brown, the librarian, as SL10473 (Sports and Leisure section).

You there yet? Right. Got it? Fact is, I'm a book – 192 pages, hardback, with a picture on the front of some geeky guy wearing pyjamas and waving his hands about.

Surprised, huh? There you were thinking that books just lay around the place, getting read and gathering dust, when up jumps old Kick and starts telling you about walking books and talking books and party dude books.

Books that now and then have had it up to here with being taken for granted. Books who decide to do something about it.

Right? Right.

Now shut up and listen.

Picture the scene. The Weston Street Library – a small, friendly sort of place, kind of scuffed but kind of homey. In one corner there's the children's library. Along the back wall is the newspaper section. Near the door (some of the old-timers would like them *outside* the door) there's a rack of videos and tapes.

It's the end of the day, right? Miss Brown goes round switching off the lights. She hesitates for a moment.

'Night, guys,' she says quietly (we like that). Then she leaves, locking the door.

Silence. Darkness. Then, after about fifteen or twenty minutes, a sound.

'Psst.'

'Ssh!'

'Ssh yourself.'

'Has she gone?'

'Duh. Only about an hour ago.'

'Sheesh, what a day I've had.'

'Me too.'

Soon the place is alive with voices – loud, soft, rude, polite, every kind of accent. We move off our shelves, ruffle our pages, stretch our spines, go visit a friend, catch up on the news.

By the middle of the night, it's party time at the Weston Street Library. In one corner, the Enid Blytons will be having yet another of their picnics. Over there, the Roald Dahls will be preparing a stinkbomb. Maybe the Anne Fines and the Judy Blumes will get together to talk about relationships.

Me, I'll be hanging out with my two best buddies, Snog and Drill – chatting, rapping and generally shooting the breeze.

Let me introduce them to you. Snog's real name is *Love's Sweet Mystery*. She's about a million pages long and her cover shows a historical couple in a clinch (hence her nickname, which she hates, by the way).

Drill is big, fat, heavy and kind of dull-looking (though no one's dared tell him this to his front cover). His real name is *The Complete A-to-Z Companion to Basic Home Decorating*.

OK, so we're kind of an odd bunch, but then friends are like that, right? Sometimes you seem to have nothing in common with your buddies except the fact that you like each other.

*

Let me tell you what brought Snog, Drill and me together. We have this one thing in common: when we're taken out by readers, each of us has a tough time.

Take Drill. Because the guy's a bit tubby (488 pages and big with it), there always comes a moment when his reader will use him to stand on. Or to prop up a work bench. Now and then he's even been used as a hammer.

With Snog, it's different. She gets the nicely-spoken ladies. By Chapter 10 (lover boy hero has to go off to war, blahdy-blah), her pages are getting a bit tear-stained. By Chapter 18 (lover boy reported killed in the war, boo-hoo), she's getting damper all the time. By the last chapter (lover boy not really killed, all a terrible mistake, comes home, hurray-hurray, kissy-kissy, happy ever after), she's awash. I tell you, sometimes when Snog gets back to her shelf, she looks as if she's been dropped in the municipal swimming-pool.

And me? Have you any idea what it's like being *Karate for Kids*? They take you home. They read you, they study you, they learn that, before a person tries breaking a brick with their bare hands, that person should always practise on something softer. Hm, something softer, eh? You can almost hear the brain ticking (face it, I don't get the brightest readers). Then, at last, they get it.

They lay me down carefully, so that I'm like a bridge between two other books.

I brace myself.

*Hiiiii-YAH!*

Crunch! Right down my spine. It's not the discomfort I mind (hey, they don't call us hardbacks for nothing), it's the ingratitude. The better I've taught them, the more they hurt me. Go figure.

So it's the Kick-Snog-Drill gang, right? Now and then we josh each other about things – Drill being a bit slow, Snog whiffing of her readers' cheap perfume, or me talking in a kind of phoney American accent (I was printed in Colchester, but my soul belongs to Colorado) but, at the end of the day when the lights go down, we're there for each other.

And we needed to be, the day they decided to close down the Weston Street Library.

Get this. One night, it's shutting-up time at the library. Except it doesn't shut up. And Miss Brown, who's looking even paler than usual, seems kind of agitated.

Now we've seen this look before (between you and me, she's not as quiet as she looks. Sometimes when she gets telephone calls after closing time, we hear conversations that would make your pages curl). But tonight's different.

Five minutes after closing time, she gets two visitors. One is Mrs Knights, the Chief Leisure Officer from the council. The other's a nerdy little guy in a suit they call Mr Johnson.

Mrs Knights makes small talk with Miss Brown. The geek wanders around the shelves looking like he's been forced to visit a rubbish dump. My bookish instinct tells me that this guy ain't no reader.

'Monster property,' he mutters to himself now and then. 'Monster investment opportunity.'

He returns to the desk where Mrs Knights and Miss Brown are standing.

'These will make excellent one-bedroom properties,' he says. 'Complete with luxury kitchenette and full en-suite facilities. A dream home for the young single professional person.'

All round the shelves, we're pricking up our pages. Did he just say 'Dream *home*'?

'Of course, closure of the library still has to be confirmed,' says Mrs Knights. 'We've got the public meeting tomorrow.'

Johnson laughs nastily. 'Yeah, yeah. Monster publicity exercise, then we go ahead, right?'

'This library is important.' At last Miss Brown speaks up. 'It's the only one in the area. How are people going to get books and information if it's closed down?'

'Like, get in a car and drive?' says the geek.

'What about children? What about old people?' Miss Brown seems on the point of tears. 'Isn't reading a right for them too?'

'Nah, books are old-fashioned.'

Miss Brown is about to reply but the property man is sidling up to her.

'Tell you what, darling,' he murmurs. 'Maybe we can get you a place at the front of the queue for one of the flats. Do you a monster deal, babe.'

'I don't want a monster deal,' hisses Miss Brown angrily. 'I want a library.'

'I'm sure your personal views will be listened to with great interest at tomorrow's meeting.' Mrs Knights glances at her watch impatiently. 'Now, if you'll excuse me. I've got a council meeting.'

'I wonder if I could take a few moments to make some measurements.' Old monster man has taken a tape-measure out of his pocket. 'It'll only take five minutes.'

'Of course,' says the Chief Leisure Officer. 'Would you mind, Miss Brown?'

'Mind?' Our librarian is staring into space. Something catches her eye. It's me. Cool as you like, I move an inch or so down the shelf. Suddenly, a distant smile is on Miss Brown's lips. 'No, of course, I don't mind. I'll just go and lock the side door.'

And, as she makes her way past us, we hear her mutter, 'Over to you, guys.' (Did I mention to you that Miss Brown knows about our secret lives? Sheesh, of *course* she does. Librarians understand books – that's what they *do*.)

Little geeky Johnson is down on his knees, measuring the length of one wall, whistling to himself, when we hear the side door being locked. Moments later, we see Miss Brown pass the window outside the library. The lock on the front door turns quietly.

'Monster, monster, monster, babe.' The geek snaps his notebook shut, stands up and looks around him. 'Babe? Miss Brown?'

He walks to the side door. As he rattles the lock unsuccessfully, one of the guys in the wildlife section – maybe *The Hodder Book of European Birds*, but I'm not sure – takes wing. Silent as an owl in flight, he floats across the room – and bangs into the light switches on the far wall.

Johnson returns to a library in darkness. 'Yeah, great joke, Miss Brown.' There's a hint of panic in his voice. 'Hit the lights, babe. I'm monster afraid of the dark.'

No reply. Bumping into shelves, swearing to himself, he edges his way to the front door. He turns the handle. Pulls the door with increasing desperation. For what seems like several minutes, he hammers on the heavy wooden door.

It's when he stops that he first becomes aware that he's not alone.

Drill makes the first move. Fact is, it's about the only move he can make but right now it works the trick big-time. He leans back on his shelf, and lets himself fall to the floor.

*Bang*!

'Who's that?' Johnson's voice is a squawk. He starts to blunder towards the window – then stops.

Like a marching army, the whole encyclopedia section makes its way out of Reference and ranges itself across the floor, barring his passage.

'Monster weird, man.' Johnson backs away, his eyes wide with alarm. 'Aagh, what was that?'

*The Hodder Book of European Birds* has taken wing again, fluttering past his face. As he turns, Snog surprises us all by scurrying across the floor, tripping him as she goes.

In the darkness, we watch Johnson crawling on his hands and knees. For some reason, I find myself thinking of all the times my readers have practised their karate chops on me. That's the thing with me – I can resist anything but temptation.

'Whack!' I swoop down and catch him a superb *haichindo* kick, knocking him flat on his face.

From the shelves all around me can be heard the other books ruffling their pages. *What* had he said? Books are *old-fashioned*? It was time Mr Johnson experienced a bit of book-learning at first hand.

Thirty minutes or so later, Johnson manages to reach the central desk and telephones the police.

By the time the cops have opened up the library, we're back on our shelves, innocent as pie.

And Johnson? They find him under a table. His suit's torn, his eyes are darting this way and that. He seems to be having trouble speaking.

'What exactly is the trouble, sir?' asks one of the policemen.

After a few seconds, he finds the words. 'M-m-m-monster books,' he whispers.

'Yes, of course, sir.' The policeman helps him to his feet. 'Books are rather monster, aren't they? I like a good read myself.'

Fast forward. The next evening, Weston Street Library is full of chairs and the chairs are full of people. I catch sight of several of Snog's whiffy ladies, maybe one or two of Drill's DIY experts. There are even some of my readers, cracking their knuckles as Mrs Knights, Johnson and Miss Brown take their places.

Mrs Knights makes a little speech. No more money, yahdy-yah, cuts in council spending, yahdy-yah, lots of other libraries in the borough, yahdy-yahdy-yah.

'But you know what they say.' She smiles brightly. 'When one door closes, another one opens.' She turns to Johnson. 'I'd like to introduce you all to the the council's property consultant, Gavin Johnson. He's going to tell you all how these premises will help another important area for the borough – housing.'

Johnson gets to his feet. 'Thank you, Mrs Knights,' he says politely. He looks around him and, in that moment, there isn't a book in the room that's not thinking that we've failed – the geek is back to his own self.

'Let me put it this way', he says. 'What does this borough need most? Monster savings in its budget and superbly designed one-bedroom flats in the brand new Library Apartment Block, or a load of mouldy old books that you can find down the road in one of the other libraries or in a bookshop?'

There are mutterings from the readers in front of him.

'The answer, of course, is books.' He sits down quickly.

For a few seconds, there's an astonished silence in the library.

Mrs Knights is the first to react. 'I *beg* your pardon?' she says. 'You're meant to be our property consultant. What about the kitchenettes, the full en-suite facilities?'

Johnson shrugs and gives a slightly embarrassed smile. 'Last night I spent a bit of quality time with the books in the library,' he says. 'I've had a monster change of mind. To tell the truth, this place would never have made very good flats anyway.'

I've never seen Miss Brown look so happy. 'Does this mean the library will stay open?' she asks.

Arms crossed, Mrs Knights is still staring at Johnson. 'It rather looks as if it will,' she murmurs.

Suddenly there's applause from all around the room. Readers of all ages are smiling with relief, Miss Brown is blushing, even old Mrs Knights and Mr Johnson seem to be enjoying their rare moment of popularity as if, in their heart of hearts, they know that the right decision has been made.

And, if you listen very carefully, you might just hear some other sounds.

Like Drill riffling his big pages in approval.

Like Snog sniffing emotionally.

Like, maybe even your old pal Kick, the hardest hardback in Weston Street Library, stretching his spine in celebration. Tell the truth, I'm kind of choked up right now just thinking about it.

And, hey, why not?

Books are people too, right?

# Gone Fishing
## Jean Richardson

It was stupid, William thought, dressing up in old clothes and pretending to be living in the past.

'Living history,' Mrs Butler had called it, when she told the class about the outing. 'We'll be going by coach' – cheers and groans – 'to Bardon Hall. It's an old house with a very interesting history' – more groans – 'and you'll be finding out what it was like, once upon a time, to live and work there.'

William liked days out. They were better than being at school, and sometimes they went to quite interesting places. Things happened too, like when Malcolm, who was very greedy, threw up in the coach, and one of the girls fainted. And there was the time at the zoo when Sandra fell into the penguin pool, and he'd gone off by himself, not known the time and kept everyone waiting. Becca, who always knew everything, claimed he'd been eaten by a lion.

William hadn't wasted much time on the lion, which looked so mangy and bad-tempered it probably would have eaten someone, given half a chance. He'd made for the small mammal house, where he peered into dimly lit windows at animals who only came out when it was dark. It was a pity there wouldn't be a small mammal house at Bardon Hall.

But there was water. As the coach crossed a grey stone bridge, William saw on either side an expanse of water so wide that there were small islands in it. He wished at once that he'd brought his rod, though Mrs Butler would probably have made him leave it behind.

He'd only just started fishing. His grandfather had bought him a rod and the two of them would sit for hours

in companionable silence on the banks of the local canal.
They didn't catch much, and usually threw back anything
they did because the fish weren't worth eating and
William hated killing things. He didn't even like the way
the fish squirmed in his hand as he freed them.

What he enjoyed was the waiting and watching, the
gradual awareness of nature, the stalking of a cunning
and elusive prey. It was a popular sport, and on a Sunday
morning they had to get there early to get a good place.
But there was no one fishing here and the water looked
very inviting. I bet there are some really big fish, William
thought. If I were a fish, it's the sort of place I'd like
to live.

The coach park was some way from the house. They
tumbled out into the sunshine and Mrs Butler led them
along a gravel path and paused by a small building.

'Does anyone want the lavatories, before we go into
the house? Sandra?' Sandra was well known for always
wanting to go when there wasn't a toilet in sight.

A few of the boys and most of the girls disappeared.
'Can we go and see the river?' William asked.

'Perhaps, if there's time. But there are lots of other
things to see first, and it's not very near the house.'

'I'd rather see the river,' William insisted. 'It's *natural*
history. Doesn't that count?'

'Y-es. I'll bear it in mind,' said Mrs Butler, secretly glad
that the river was not near. Twenty-five children and
unfenced water could be a problem.

When everyone was ready, she led them through the
turreted gatehouse, across the courtyard, up some steps
and into the magnificent Great Hall. It had an ornate
ceiling miles above them and a vast fireplace with a gilded
coat-of-arms.

'Welcome to Bardon,' said a grey-haired lady wearing a
Trust badge on her lapel. 'I'd like to tell you a little about
the Bardon family and their house before we go

downstairs and step into the past. Now the house was built . . . '

William stopped listening. Bars of sunlight slotted through the shutters and by moving to the edge of the group he could just see the river. He wondered how one got out to the islands. There was probably a rowing boat or a dinghy. He could paddle a dinghy and his grandfather had promised to teach him to row.

' . . . and I'll be telling you more about the family as we go round the house. Now let's go and find your clothes.'

The Trust lady led them down a flight of stone stairs and into one of the kitchens. 'We got you the clothes you'd have worn if you'd joined the household in 1820,' she said. 'You'd probably have grown up in one of the estate cottages and known the Bardon family all your life. You might have been taken on to help in the garden, or the stables, or the kitchen, or upstairs. A house this size took a lot of looking after. Now perhaps you'd like to get dressed.'

William took his time, hoping that there might not be enough clothes to go round. He hated the idea of dressing up. If he had to be someone in the past, why couldn't it be someone who went fishing.

The girls got changed amid squeaks and cries of 'Do me up' and 'How does this go?'. They wore long dresses of sprigged patterns, crisp white aprons and frilly caps. Everyone began to look different. Lucy twirled her skirt in front of William and he found himself blushing. He liked Lucy.

'Aren't you going to change?' she asked teasingly. A curl had escaped from her cap and William noticed that her eyes were very blue.

'There aren't enough things to go round,' he said lamely.

'Miss, William hasn't got any clothes,' said Becca, ever the busybody.

William glared at her. Her cap made her look daft.

The Trust lady came over. 'Have you looked in that box in the corner? I'm sure we counted correctly.'

William moved reluctantly towards the box. He didn't fancy being a gardener's boy, a stable lad or a footman. The box was empty, but the woman was talking to her assistant and they would obviously find him something. Probably something awful.

And then he saw the clothes. They were lying on a chair as though someone had just taken them off, and they looked reassuringly normal. True, the shirt had a stupid frilly collar, but the fawn trousers and dark jacket weren't too bad.

By the time William had got dressed, the room was empty. He thought he could hear the Trust lady explaining something nearby, but there was no one in the corridor outside. He walked along looking for the others, but they seemed to have disappeared. Then he saw a couple of boys ahead and ran to join them.

'There you are,' said one crossly. 'We've been looking for you everywhere.' They were both wearing clothes like his, but they weren't boys from his class. He couldn't remember whether Mrs Butler had said any other schools were taking part.

'Luke wants to go fishing,' said the smaller boy. 'What do you think?'

William stared at them. The Trust woman hadn't said anything about going fishing. 'Can we?' he asked. 'I didn't bring my rod.'

'Well, go and get it,' said the other boy, just as though they were both at home.

'It's in the gun-room,' chipped in the smaller boy. 'You put it back there last time.'

William didn't know what to say. It seemed that as well as dressing up, they were expected to pretend they actually lived here. These two were very good at it. William bet they were good at writing stories too.

'Come on,' said the taller boy. 'You and Matthew get the rods and I'll go and scrounge some food. I expect I can persuade Dorcas to let us have a couple of pies and apples.' And he stalked off.

He knows how to act the part, William thought admiringly. And Matthew seemed to know his way about the house. He had no problem negotiating the maze of corridors that led to the gun-room.

It looked more like a sports shop than a room in a private house. William fingered a superb rod, wondering if he could manage it. Then he caught Matthew's eye. 'Not Father's,' Matthew said disapprovingly. 'There'll be the most awful row.'

William put the rod back. 'Where's mine?' he said, pretending to look round.

'Here, you duffer,' said Matthew, handing him a far more modest rod. 'Can you carry Luke's too, and I'll take the basket.' He put some flies into a small wicker basket and led the way out into the courtyard.

There was no one about. William wondered where the rest of the class was. The clock above the stable chimed the hour. Was it twelve o'clock already? He hoped no one else would turn up. Three was just the right number for fishing.

Luke joined them. 'Game pie, cheese and apples,' he said. 'Dorcas wasn't there, so I helped myself.'

A bit cool, William thought, but he didn't like to say so. Presumably, it was all part of living history.

The three boys crossed the courtyard and set off for the river.

The class were now in one of the state bedrooms. The boys were impatient to reach the armoury, where they were to try on a suit of armour, but the girls wanted to take turns on the fourposter where a queen had once slept.

'The curtains are over two hundred years old,' said the Trust lady. 'They didn't have central heating in those days, but the bed curtains helped to keep out the draught.'

Lucy climbed onto the bed. It wasn't very comfortable. The curtains smelled of a mixture of lavender and the dust of hundreds of crumbled-away years. Lucy shivered and was about to scramble off the bed when the curtains began to waver. She felt herself struggling for breath. Some force was driving the air out of her lungs. As she tried to fight against it, she realized that it was water. She was drowning. She tried to push up towards the surface, but her legs and feet were entangled in ropes of weed that held her down. She thrashed out with her arms, straining to free herself, as a sudden shaft of sunlight pierced her watery grave.

'Are you all right?' The Trust lady looked concerned. 'Take some deep breaths. It can get a little claustrophobic with the curtains drawn.'

'You look as though you've seen a ghost,' said Becca. 'Are there any ghosts, miss?'

The Trust lady hesitated. 'I don't think so,' she said, 'but there was a tragic death in the family. I'll tell you about it later.'


Luke led the way to the boathouse, where a small rowing boat was moored. Matthew jumped in and seized the oars. 'Your turn to bale,' he said to William. 'Jennings hasn't done anything about the leak yet.'

William sat down in the stern. The water in the bottom of the boat looked like cold tea. He began scooping it out with a tin cup, while Luke cast off.

'Let's go downstream,' he said. 'Jennings'll look for us at Merlin's Pool. He'll never guess we've gone the other way.'

Jennings must be the teacher in charge of their class, William thought. He wondered if Mrs Butler had noticed

he was missing, but he didn't care. This was much better than being stuck indoors.

The sun shone full on the water, creating a golden haze. Here and there trailing branches combed the water that sucked gently round the holes where riverbank creatures lived. A moorhen bobbed up and down on the waves created by Matthew, who was hauling expertly on the oars. William hoped Luke wouldn't ask him to take a turn. He didn't want to admit that he couldn't row.

'There's a lot of dragonflies about,' said Luke, as a flash of blue and green darted across the boat.

'Let's stop soon,' said Matthew, whose face was red with exertion. He'd slung his jacket down beside William and the sleeves trailed in the water sloshing around in the bottom. William wondered if they'd get into trouble if they damaged the clothes.

'How about here?' said Luke. 'Grab that branch, William.'

I didn't tell him my name, thought William, but the puzzle went out of his head as a low branch hit him and he fell forward amid a scuffle of leaves.

The Trust lady had stopped in front of a large painting at the top of the stairs. It showed three boys who had just come back from fishing. The eldest was holding the rods and the youngest had a wicker basket in which he had put their catch, but it was the middle boy who caught Lucy's attention. He was the spitting image of William.

She looked round to check, but there was no sign of William. She realized that she hadn't seen him since they'd teased him about the clothes.

The Trust lady was taking about the picture. ' . . . three brothers. As you can see, they were fond of fishing, but shortly after this picture was painted, there was a tragic accident and the middle brother, William, was drowned. It seems that the boys had gone downstream and their boat was swept over the weir. William wasn't a strong swimmer and the other boys couldn't save him. He was about your age, so don't be tempted to take any risks. The river may look lovely, but it's a very dangerous place.'

It was one of the best meals William had ever had. He was still doubtful about the value of living history, but there was nothing wrong with eating it. There was nothing musty about the game pie, strong cheese and crisp apples. They seemed to have more flavour than anything he'd eaten for ages. But perhaps the setting improved the taste: the deserted stretch of water, occasionally ruffled by some creature hurrying past; the excitement of a pull on his rod; the companionship of Luke and Matthew. He felt as though he'd known them all his life, though they'd only exchanged a few words.

He crunched into another apple and stared out into the dazzling sunlight. He'd forgotten to put on his watch that morning, and neither Luke nor Matthew wore watches. They didn't seem to worry about the time, so why should he . . .

The class were picnicking on the lawn. They'd changed back into their school clothes and were their normal selves, popping crisp packets and blowing bubbles in tins of cola. Only Lucy didn't want her sandwiches and had given them to Malcolm. She'd not been able to find William, nor persuade Mrs Butler that he was in any danger.

'Has anyone seen William Turner?' Mrs Butler asked. No one had. 'I expect he got lost in the house,' she said to the student teacher who had offered to keep an eye on the class. 'Could you tell Mrs Spence, the Trust lady, we're missing one. It's probably his idea of a joke.'

The student teacher went up to the house to alert Mrs Spence while Mrs Butler stretched out on the grass and told herself not to worry. What harm could come to a child on such a perfect day. They were lucky to have such marvellous weather . . .

It was Luke who finally suggested a move. They'd each caught several small fish that they killed and then put in the wicker basket. William wanted to throw his back, but Luke wouldn't let him.

'We've eaten smaller ones than this,' he said, 'and we can always give them to the cats.' Matthew had killed his, so William gave in. He didn't want to spoil a perfect day.

'Let's go downstream,' suggested Matthew. 'We've never been further than this.'

Luke took the oars and shoved off from the bank. He pulled strongly and the boat sped through the water which ran in swift ribbons through William's fingers as he trailed his hand over the side. He wondered if he would see Luke and Matthew again, and if he could ask Luke to teach him to row.

The river was hastening them along, and William though he could hear a distant roar, as though somewhere ahead the water became more powerful . . .

The student teacher and Mrs Spence had searched the house from top to bottom but found no sign of William.

'He went off once before,' said Mrs Butler, 'when we went to the zoo. The boy is rather a loner.' She'd established that no one had seen William since they'd changed into their costumes, and she'd had to be firm with Lucy, who had some extraordinary idea that William had got into a painting and was going to be drowned. Lucy had refused the ride in a horse-drawn carriage but had been persuaded to sit under a tree with Becca, who was enjoying the drama.

'I'll get a couple of gardeners to search the grounds,' said Mrs Spence. 'The boy's probably wandered off and got lost. He could be in the maze.'

But William wasn't found until the class had gone back with the student teacher, leaving a now distraught Mrs Butler to raise the alarm. Teams of local people, organized by the police, began combing the gardens, the woodland and the river bank.

William's body was found floating in the water on the far side of the weir. It was presumed that he had fallen in, though it was not clear how he managed to be so far from the house. The other mystery was his clothes. All the costumes used for the living history project had been specially made by a local firm from modern fabric. But at the inquest an expert witness from a costume museum swore that William's clothes were about a hundred and seventy years old.

# Dan, Dan the Half-Time Man
## Janet Burchett and Sara Vogler

'That Dan – he's so slow a tortoise could tackle him.'

'And he'd be so long getting out of the changing room he'd meet the team coming back.'

'Yeah, and if he did a circuit of the pitch he'd have to take his pyjamas.'

Dan Craddock tried to shrink down in his seat at the back of the school bus – which was hard for a boy who was as round as the oranges he handed out at half-time. Dan was the largest and most devoted fan of West Oldfield Road Sunday Team. Chaz Patel, their manager, had appointed him team caterer and physiotherapist. It was a posh name for the boy who cuts up oranges and splashes wet sponges about. Football was Dan's life. He would have given anything to be in the team, even if it was only as Harry the Substitute's substitute. And then maybe one magnificent day . . .

'. . . *And it's Craddock. He receives a good ball. He hits it strongly . . . and knocks it in! That's his hat trick. They've only been on the pitch four minutes . . .*'

As the commentator's voice faded, Dan could still hear Sidney Trump and his mate broadcasting his skills to the whole bus. Blaring it out like the loudspeaker at Wembley.

Dan listened to the sniggers. No-one was shouting about Sid and his only attempt at goal last Sunday. No-one was shouting about the ball hitting the woodwork and bouncing straight back to Sid's feet. Sid had been so busy celebrating his near miss he didn't notice it.

'Even I could have scored from there,' thought Dan.

Still, he was entitled to wear the West Oldfield Road Sunday Team sweatshirt. He wore it with pride. Sadly, no-one had realized what the initials spelt until the shirts came back from the printers: WORST FC. And they were. They were the worst in the Sunday league. They were so bad their dads didn't even bother to fight on the touchline any more. For as long as anyone could remember they'd come fifteenth. There were fifteen teams in the league.

That Sunday, Dan chopped oranges into neat wedges.

'What a waste of time,' he thought. 'Oranges don't make goals. We haven't scored for fifty-eight matches.'

Chaz was giving his pre-match talk. 'I want my team to play total football. I want us to play a passing game, balls to feet. And Tracy – boots on the right feet this week. Let's be getting up into their penalty area . . . '

Dan looked around the motley crew that were the team. They had trouble getting up in the morning.

' . . . I want the defence to move out as one and that's down to you, Gita. If they play the offside game, we do the same. I want total commitment from everybody. And don't pick your nose on the pitch, Vince.'

The team looked about as lively as a row of last year's turnips. They didn't believe they could win any more. Dan was worried they were going to break up and where would that leave him? He wasn't even good enough for a free transfer. An orange squirted in his eye. He couldn't see the point in having oranges. All the players did was have a quick slurp and toss them to the ground. What a way to treat his little segments.

Then an idea kicked off in his brain and ran up the wing. Play began, but he was so busy thinking that he didn't see Gita's clumsy tackle that gave the other side a penalty. He was so busy thinking, he didn't notice Jim the Goalie tread on his own boot-laces as he tried to save the penalty. He was so busy thinking, he barely heard Sid's vicious comments as he lumbered on to the pitch with his plate at half-time. He'd got it! The idea bounced twice round his skull and hit the back of the net. He couldn't wait to get home.

Everyone was out so he had the kitchen to himself. He was going to concoct something. Something to wake them up. Something to make them win.

He experimented all afternoon. He like the colour of the lemon and mustard drink but felt it might be a touch too lively. The jam and tomato sauce tasted OK but Jim the Goalie always fainted at the sight of blood. Especially as it was usually his.

'If I can get this right,' thought Dan, 'it might even work on me.' He pictured the scene.

' . . . *And it's Craddock. What a run this boy has made. Craddock on his left foot, still Craddock. He's leaving the defenders standing. He won't shoot from there, will he? No . . . Yes, he has! My word, what a goal! This boy is destined for the premiership . . .*'

Dan came back to earth with a burp. He was feeling sick. He couldn't bring himself to try the cayenne pepper and sprout purée – it might cause some explosive runs. In the end, apple juice and marmalade were the only jars he hadn't opened. It could work. He'd try it on the team next Sunday.

'What's this?' snarled Sid. 'Where's me orange? Footballers always have oranges.'

'It's apple juice with a hint of marmalade.'

'Don't like the bits in marmalade,' said Gita.

'It'll give you energy for the second half,' said Dan, encouragingly.

Jim the Goalie had a taste. 'This is good,' he said. 'The bitterness of the peel contrasting subtly with the sweet autumnal flavours of the apple.'

The others risked a sip. They had seconds. Sid had thirds.

The team seemed unusually lively as they ran out for the second half.

Dan wondered if his drink was working already. WORST FC kicked off. Gita took the ball up the wing. She crossed to Sid who, for a change, saw the ball coming and was in the right position. It was a great pass.

'It must be the drink,' thought Dan. 'We don't usually keep possession for more than thirty seconds.'

The opposition were not prepared for this – WORST FC on the attack! Sid had plenty of room. He drilled the ball into the back of the net.

WORST FC's seven supporters were too stunned to cheer. Chaz Patel stood gobsmacked.

'It's working!' yelled Dan.

It took the referee some time to disentangle the players from their celebratory scrum.

Then WORST FC were on the attack again! Gita passed to Vince. Vince on towards Sid. Sid ran with the ball. It could be another goal. He was about to shoot when suddenly he crumpled. He crossed his legs and groaned with pain. The referee blew his whistle.

'I never touched him,' yelled the big defender.

Dan ran on with his sponge. Chaz and Harry the Substitute were close behind.

'I'm not hurt,' panted Sid. 'I'm just busting!'

He winced off to the loo. Tracy followed, then Gita, then Jim the Goalie. Five minutes later there were only three of their team left on the pitch – and they looked pale.

WORST FC lost eleven–one.

'We should have stuck to oranges,' hissed Sid.

But Dan knew it would work – if he got the formula right. After all, they'd scored a goal. Something less liquidy was called for. He flicked through his recipe book. Rock cakes? Sausage rolls? Toffee . . . ? Toffee! Made with

skimmed milk. It would be energizing but not heavy – and at least they'd stick on the pitch.

Next Sunday they were three down at half-time. The team groaned when they saw Dan's plate of toffees.

'I want me orange,' moaned Sid.

'Now, team,' said Chaz. 'That was a first half that simmered rather than boiled. Remember last week. Remember the goal. Forget what happened after. Focus on that goal. Let's keep right bang up there. Anyone need the loo?' Without thinking he took a toffee. 'Mmmmn,' he grinned.

Jim the Goalie had a lick. 'It's energizing but there's no hint of the heaviness you normally associate with toffee.' He started chewing.

They all had one.

They were till chewing when the second half started. Finchley Avenue Sunday Team swept out from defence.

'Markammmm!' yelled Jim the Goalie.

Chaz tried to shout instructions from the bench. 'Brghmh!' he garbled. 'Lookagoogoo!'

The striker dodged round Vince, who was attempting to force his jaws apart. He whizzed past Gita, who had her finger stuck to a tooth. Jim the Goalie was too busy getting toffee out of his molars with his goalkeeper gloves. *Smack!* The ball hit the back of the net.

They lost thirteen–nil.

When Chaz finally removed the toffee from his teeth, he didn't have the heart to blame Dan.

'We were always in the game,' he said.

Sid tripped Dan up as he went past.

Desperate, Dan decided to have one last go for their home match against Trafford Old Place FC next Sunday. Then he'd go back to the oranges. One last attempt to find something refreshing without bladder problems.

Taste without lockjaw. Something that was light and invigorating. He looked in his recipe book.

On Sunday, Trafford Old Place were two–nil up at half-time.

Dan pulled back the tea towel to reveal his fluffy white creations.

'Not again,' snarled Sid.

Chaz looked nervous. He'd been at the dentist for three hours on Monday.

'You first,' said Gita to Tracy.

'After you,' said Vince to Harry the Substitute.

Jim the Goalie took a mini-meringue. He stared at it long and hard and then shoved it quickly in his mouth. The others watched anxiously as he chewed. 'Delicious,' he said. 'It's airy with a refreshing liquid centre. Orange and honey, I believe. Light and invigorating.'

As Jim the Goalie could still speak, the others fell upon the mini-meringues. They even squabbled over the last one before racing on to the pitch for the second half.

Jim the Goalie had a system. He would dive to the right three times and then to the left three times, unless it was a leap year. Occasionally he connected with the ball. Today he got it right. He saw the striker bearing down on him. He dived to the left and the ball slammed into his belly. As he creased up in pain he found his arms clutching the ball. It was an amazing save.

'The boy done brilliant!' gasped Chaz. 'I can't bear to watch.'

And he didn't. Dan and Harry the Substitute commentated for him. It was an exciting second half. Jim the Goalie's save, or the meringues, or something had turned it into a different ball game.

'Tracy's got the ball now,' said Dan. 'That's a good touch to Sid.'

'He's gone wide,' continued Harry the Substitute. 'He's crossed it. No, it was too deep.'

'But Gita's picked it up. She's breaking out to the right. She's ridden a tackle – and she's gone for goal . . . '

Chaz peeped through his fingers.

'She's beaten the goalie,' shrieked Dan. 'Ohhh! She's been denied by the crossbar.'

'And it's Sid,' screamed Harry the Substitute. 'He's seeking out Tracy. She's spotted the ball. She's let fly . . . it's a goal!'

The bench leapt in the air.

'West Oldfie-ld,' chanted the nine fans.

'Two–one!' whispered Chaz.

Suddenly there was a tiny chance they might not lose – and the team smelt it.

Vince took the ball down the wing. He dodged a defender but the ball went out of play. It was a Trafford Old Place throw. Gita intercepted and flicked it to Vince. He found Tracy. Then on to Sid. It was a great first touch. It was a great finish. The final whistle blew – two–all.

So every Sunday Dan prepared his little meringues. All the team, even Sid, gave orders for their favourite fillings but sometimes he surprised them with a new taste.

The last game of the season was an away fixture at East Village Lane FC. They were fourteenth in the league. Critics said they'd do better if their players stayed on the pitch. But EVIL FC aimed for an average of three red cards per game. This was the critical match.

'If we win,' said Chaz, 'we'll be off the bottom. A dream come true.'

Dan had prepared two trays of meringues. He felt the team needed that extra something. Pre-match . . . strawberry and vanilla.

'What's for half-time?' asked Vince, his mouth full.

'Wait and see,' said Dan. He was feeling good. Even Sid was nice to him now. Other teams had heard about his secret recipe. Trafford Old Place had tried to poach him. They'd even promised him a game now and then. But Dan remained loyal to WORST FC.

Dastardly plans were being hatched in East Village Lane's changing room.

'Something's happened to West Oldfield,' said Virginia Jones. 'I think they're on atomic steroids.'

'Nah,' said Blades Wilkinson, 'it's them sweets.'

'I'm not being beaten by WORST FC,' snarled Erica the Red Card.

'I'll leave you to sort it,' said McThuggart the manager, with a horrible wink.

Erica the Red Card nobbled Vince with a sliding tackle. He limped off to the changing room. Erica got her red card and joined McThuggart on the bench, just as she'd planned.

'On you go, son.' Chaz pushed a reluctant Harry the Substitute forward. 'Remember, look for that loose ball – and try to keep your shorts up.'

Ten minutes before half-time, Dan was passed a note.

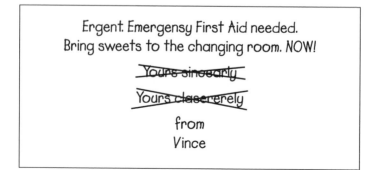

Dan rushed into the building.

Suddenly hands covered his eyes. Someone snatched his tray. He was pushed into a dark cupboard. He heard the key turn. He hammered at the door. He shouted, but everyone was on the pitch.

There was a small window high up. Dan climbed on the shelves and tried to squeeze through. He had to get his meringues back The team depended on him.

'Where's Dan?' asked Sid at half-time.

'Where's my meringue?' asked Jim the Goalie.

Chaz Patel took charge. 'You'll be all right, you've had a pre-match sweet. Vince, go and find Dan.' Vince limped off. 'Now, Gita, watch out for Ginnie Jones. Let's defend deep. Let's play tight. We've held them to nil–nil. Just focus on that fourteenth place.'

Chaz was right. The match was the thing. But was one meringue going to be enough?

Dan was stuck. Stuck in the tiny window. He shouted and screamed. Surely someone would come along.

East Village Lane stuffed their faces with Dan's lemon sherbet meringues. Dan had been experimenting. He thought lemon sherbet might give the team more fizz. He was right. Every thirty seconds, an EVIL FC player would clutch their belly and belch. Loudly.

'I feel as sick as a parrot,' groaned Ginnie Jones.

Tracy dazzled the burping defenders with her dribbling. She darted forwards and feinted to the right. She lofted the ball across to Sid, who had come fast down the wing. Sid volleyed it back to Tracy. She sprang into the air and headed the ball into the net. The seventeen WORST FC fans did a Mexican wave. Their team was one–nil up.

Ginnie Jones had had enough. When the ref wasn't looking she head-butted Tracy.

Chaz rushed on with Dan's sponge. 'How many fingers am I holding up?' he asked her anxiously.

'Half-past two,' said Tracy. She wandered off the pitch.

Stuck in his window Dan had heard the roar from the crowd. EVIL FC must have scored. Then he saw Tracy tottering along.

'Tracy!' he shouted. 'Give us a hand.'

'Right at the lights,' said Tracy. She turned left and disappeared. Then Vince limped by.

'Hi, Dan,' he called. 'Seen Tracy? The ambulance is here.'

'She went that way . . . Hey, Vince!' But Vince had gone.

At last, to his relief, Chaz ran up. He struggled to get Dan free.

'You didn't have to go into hiding,' he said. 'It's not that bad. We're one–nil up . . . '

'No,' began Dan. 'It was EVIL FC. They . . . '

But Chaz wasn't listening. ' . . . It's not that good either,' he continued. 'Tracy's off the field with concussion. I need you to play.'

Dan's dream was coming true. He was going to take to the field as a member of West Oldfield Road Sunday Team. And he could do it. He was goal-hungry.

Dan lumbered on to the pitch. He jogged up and down in his own half. He was about to do some press-ups when the ball rolled towards him. He was going to get his first touch! EVIL FC were down to nine players but they looked like ninety as they advanced on him. Panicking he swung his foot hard and there was the ball, in the back of the net. His own net.

Suddenly the dark cupboard seemed like a good place to be.

Dan was angry. Angry with himself for messing up, and angry with EVIL FC. He ran towards a hiccuping Blades Wilkinson who had possession. Blades swayed to the left and thought he had sold Dan a dummy but found the ball had gone. Dan didn't know how he'd done it. He tried to pass to Harry the Substitute on his left. It reached Gita on his right.

''Ere we go,' sang the fans.

The defenders fell back, burping, to pack the goal area. They looked ugly – and their mood wasn't good either.

'Come on, team,' yelled Chaz. 'It's not over till it's over.'

Gita made a perfect through ball to Sid but he was boxed in. He back-heeled it to land at Dan's feet. Dan trapped the ball in the curve of his left foot. He steadied it and then blasted a shot at goal. It bounced off a defender. Corner! Harry the Substitute took it. He chipped the ball into the penalty area. Sid pounced. He hammered it towards the goal. It hit the goalkeeper, who was belching and hanging weakly from the goal-post. Dan ran forwards to get into the action but tripped over his own feet. *Thump!* He collided with something and hit the ground as the final whistle went.

He lifted his mud-stained face to see the whole team coming towards him. He had let them down. He'd had his sweets stolen and he'd scored an own goal. But Sid and Harry the Substitute were grinning. They dragged him to his feet. Jim the Goalie kissed him!

'That was some header,' said Gita.

'The goalie didn't stand a chance!' yelled Sid.

They tried to lift him on to their shoulders and collapsed in a heap. Vince's and Gita's dads started fighting with the elation of it all.

'Dan, Dan, the half-time man!' chanted the fans.

Dan suddenly realized he had scored the winning goal. WORST FC had begun to climb up the league.

On Monday, Sid Trump and his mate could be heard all over the school bus.

'Obviously, we was well made up.'

'Think Dan'll be in the team now?'

'Yeah. He may be slow but he's got a wicked head.'

Dan sat proudly at the back of the school bus.

# The Amazing Mr Endicott
## Eric Brown

Mr Endicott was one hundred years old that week. Imagine that. *One hundred!*

He was born in the last century, in 1897. Although he was ninety years older than me, he was still fit and active. He walked ten miles a day just for fun. He had a photographic memory – he never forgot anything he ever saw, heard or read. His cottage next door was like a museum, stuffed with a thousand fascinating objects collected on his travels around the world.

But the most important thing about Mr Endicott was that he was my best friend.

'What's the Diplomatic Service?' I once asked my mum.

'It means the civil servants who work for the Government in foreign countries.'

'Mr Endicott worked for the Diplomatic Service,' I said. 'He told me he was posted to a dozen different countries.' I thought about that. I was only six at the time. 'But how did they find an envelope big enough?'

Mum laughed and told me that being posted to another country meant being sent overseas to work.

Even so, I grew up thinking that Mr Endicott was magical, some kind of wizard who climbed into giant envelopes and popped out – *hey presto!* – in hot and dusty countries!

But the truth was even stranger . . .

One week before his hundredth birthday party, I went for a long walk with Mr Endicott.

Every week he set off across the moors with his knapsack full of sardine sandwiches and a flask of coffee.

Mum packed a lunch in my Power Ranger lunch-box and I joined him.

Over the years he had told me a hundred amazing stories – about his life in distant countries, the strange and wonderful things he had seen and experienced.

But today he was quiet as he strode up the hillside above the village. Perhaps he was contemplating the fact that he was almost one hundred years old.

We paused at the top of the hill and looked around us at the rolling moorland and our village nestling in the valley.

He pointed at the horizon with his stick. 'Over this way, Tommy. I want to show you something.'

One hour later we stopped on the crest of a hill and stared across the vale. It looked like every other stretch of moorland we'd crossed that morning.

We sat on a rock, munched our lunch and drank our coffee.

Mr Endicott mopped his face with a big white handkerchief. 'Did I ever tell you that I was born in Holbury?' he asked.

Holbury was a small town a mile from my village. I shook my head. As far as I could recall, he had never mentioned where he came from.

'Well, I was. A hundred years ago next week. Seems like just yesterday that I was a lad your age, playing on the moors . . . ' He paused, staring into the distance, or into the distant past. 'I was a bit like you, Tommy. Curious. Happy with my own company. I'd often go wandering off by myself. Exploring. Watching the wildlife, the birds and animals that made the moors their home.'

We finished our sandwiches and set off again. I waded through the knee-high heather, the wiry plants scratching my bare legs.

At last Mr Endicott stopped and pointed at a large, circular hole in the ground before us, perhaps one metre deep.

'I've never been back here since that day,' he said to himself.

I stared at the hole. 'What is it?'

He looked at me. 'What happened here is a long story,' he told me. 'I do believe it's a two-parter.'

I smiled. Mr Endicott's stories were sometimes one-parters, tales that could be told in one afternoon, and sometimes two-parters, longer stories that took two afternoons to tell.

He turned and we set off back to the village. 'This happened a long time ago,' he said. 'And I've never told anyone about it. Never trusted anyone enough to tell them what happened. But you . . . you remind me of the boy I was, Tommy. So here's the first part.'

Mr Endicott told me that it happened in September 1907.

He was lying in bed, unable to get to sleep. Every time he drifted off, he thought he could hear a voice in his head, telling him to climb out of bed and walk onto the moors.

So he did. He obeyed the voice. He was curious. He got dressed and crept quietly downstairs and slipped out of the back door.

As he walked towards the moors, he could no longer hear the voice. But he seemed to know where to go. He left the lane and strode across the moorland.

It was a moonlit night and the heather stretched away like the waves of a vast, silver sea. He had no idea what was happening, but he was not afraid.

Then he was standing on the hillside where we had eaten our lunch, staring across the moonlit moors. Suddenly, out of the southern sky near the constellation of Orion, came a fiery ball. He stared at it, a part of him frightened at what he was seeing, but another part calm. The voice entered his head again, telling him not to panic.

Then the fiery ball did something very strange. It slowed down. As he watched, the ball lost all its fire and became a dark shape against the stars as it lowered itself slowly to the ground. The boy walked towards it as if in a trance.

'I couldn't stop myself,' Mr Endicott said now. 'I was drawn towards the object. I *had* to walk towards it. What happened next changed my life.'

I stared at him in fascination. 'What did happen next?' I gasped.

He smiled. 'Look, we're almost home. That's the end of part one. Part two is next Saturday.'

I said goodbye, my head full of his amazing tale. I wondered if I could wait a whole week to hear the second part of the story.

I lay awake for a long time that night, thinking about what Mr Endicott had told me. Just as I was falling asleep, I had an idea.

In the morning I caught a bus into town and made my way to the local newspaper office. I asked if I could look in their records department for copies of their paper from September 1907.

'You're in luck,' a junior reporter told me as we entered the cellar where all the back-issues were kept. 'The *News* was founded in 1906. Here we are, September 1907.'

He deposited a pile of old newspapers on the desk before me, then left me alone in the dusty room. For the next two hours I looked through paper after paper searching for a report about lights in the sky.

I was beginning to give up hope. I had looked through more than twenty newspapers with no luck. The dust was making me sneeze.

Then, in the last-but-one paper, I found what I was looking for. The report had three headlines, each one smaller than the last, which was the fashion in old newspapers.

# Fireball Over Holbury!
## Mystery Object Seen in Night Sky
### Experts suspect meteorite

I read: *A number of independent witnesses reported seeing a bright fireball in the night sky over the Holbury moors on the evening of the 25th. Said PC Crowther: 'It was the size of a house and fiery, and it came down on the moors a mile above the town. I investigated but discovered nothing suspicious.'*

I read other eye-witness accounts. Finally an astronomer from London gave his opinion: *It sounds very much as though your witnesses saw a meteorite, which are common at this time of the year . . .*

I left the cellar, thanked the junior reporter, and caught the bus back home.

So Mr Endicott had seen something that night, all those years ago. And, I knew, it was something much more than a meteorite. On Saturday Mr Endicott would tell me everything . . .

The week seemed to drag. I looked out for Mr Endicott, but he remained inside his cottage. I thought of paying him a visit and begging him to tell me the second part of the story, but that would have been rude. I would just have to be patient and wait.

On Saturday, the day before his birthday party, I packed some sandwiches and hurried out to meet Mr Endicott. He was waiting by his garden gate, staring into the cloudless sky. 'Wonderful day for a walk, Tommy. Fit and ready?'

'Fit and ready!' I declared, and we set off up the lane and across the moors. We strode a mile along the bridleway, then turned east towards Holbury and the strange, circular depression in the ground.

Mr Endicott talked all the way but not about what he had seen on the moors that night. He talked about his long life, his experiences in World War One. He told me about the many countries he had visited while working for the Government.

At last we arrived at the hole in the ground. We sat and ate our lunch in silence.

I asked: 'Can you tell me the second part of the story, Mr Endicott? What happened when you walked towards the fireball?'

He smiled and finished his coffee. He seemed to take a long time to pack his flask and sandwich-box into his knapsack. He stood.

'Where did I get to, Tommy? Ah, yes,' he said as we set off home. 'By the time it touched the ground, it was no longer a fireball. It was . . . it was a dark, oval shape – something like a rugby ball. Steam rose from its surface, and it hissed in the silence of the night. Oddly, I wasn't frightened.'

He told me that he walked towards the object and stopped, staring up at it in silent wonder. He saw that the thing was made of some kind of dark metal, and he could see windows or viewscreens on its upper curves. As he stared, he told himself that he could make out shapes behind those windows, small people-shapes.

What happened next took him by surprise. A section of the oval dropped down to form a kind of ramp. From inside the object a white, foul-smelling gas leaked out. He covered his nose with his hand and backed away.

Then, as he stared, he made out a small figure walking down the ramp through the mist.

'What happened then?' I asked.

'The figure approached me slowly, holding out its hand. It was small – no larger than yourself. It was dressed in a silver suit, and wore some kind of glass helmet. Behind the face-plate, I made out its features. It had two big black eyes, no nose at all, and just a slit for a mouth.'

'An alien!' I gasped.

Mr Endicott nodded. 'An alien,' he said.

'Did it attack you?'

He smiled. 'No – no, it didn't attack me. It came in peace. Of course, I was frightened to begin with. But then I heard the voice in my head, again. It told me not to be afraid, that I would not be harmed. They were a peaceful people . . . '

Mr Endicott paused. We were almost home.

'And then?' I asked.

'And then the alien reached out its long arm. It held something in its hand, something like a pistol. The voice in my head told me not to panic. I stood there, very still, and the alien touched me with its pistol. Suddenly I felt heat pass through me, and I was surrounded by light.'

We had paused outside my house – and at that very second my mum appeared at the door. 'Tommy, there you are. Afternoon, Mr Endicott. All ready for tomorrow? Come on, Tommy – it's dinner time.'

'But the rest of the story!'

'Tomorrow, Tommy,' he said. 'I'll tell you what happened, tomorrow.'

We held the party on the lawn of our back garden. All the neighbours came, and lots of dignitaries, the vicar and the Lord Mayor from town. A photographer from the local paper was there, taking shots of Mr Endicott cutting into his cake. Even a TV crew turned up and interviewed him. 'How does it feel to be one hundred years old, Mr Endicott?' the reporter asked with stunning originality. 'I must say, you do look well for your age!'

I wondered what the papers and TV would say if they knew that Mr Endicott had met an alien being!

When I found myself alone with Mr Endicott, I said, 'You said you'd tell me the end of the story today.'

He smiled at me. 'Later,' he whispered. 'When we're quite alone. I promise.'

Except, there was no later.

The party ended, and the Lord Mayor insisted on taking Mr Endicott off to an official function in town. Disappointed, I watched the Rolls Royce carry him away.

That night I could not sleep. Once I did slip off, but woke seconds later. I thought I heard a voice in my head . . .

But that was ridiculous! I must be dreaming of what had happened to Mr Endicott, back in 1907.

I climbed out of bed and stared through the window. The moon was full, illuminating the moors with its silver light. As I stared, I saw a figure.

It was Mr Endicott, standing on the skyline, and looking back at my house.

He waved at me, then turned and walked off across the moors.

I dressed as fast as I could, crept downstairs and let myself out through the back door. I ran to where I had seen Mr Endicott, and stared across the moors.

There he was, striding with determination through the heather. I gave chase, shouting his name and pleading with him to slow down.

I wondered if I was dreaming . . .

Then, high overhead, I saw the fireball. It streaked across the night sky, plummeting rapidly to earth. As I watched, its fiery tail disappeared, and the object . . . the *spaceship* . . . came to rest on the moonlit moorland.

'Mr Endicott!' I cried.

He turned. 'Tommy,' he said. 'I promised I'd tell you how it ended.'

He took my hand and together we walked towards the spaceship.

We stopped, staring.

'When the alien touched me with its pistol-device,' Mr Endicott whispered, 'I was surrounded by a bright white light, and a voice in my head explained everything. It told me that I would never fall ill, that cuts and bruises would quickly heal. That I would live on Earth to be a hundred. In here,' he tapped his chest, 'I have never aged. And my memory – that, too, was a gift from the aliens.'

'But why? Why did they help you like this?'

'The voice told me that they would return for me when I was one hundred years old. They would take me to their home among the stars, where other humans like me live. You see, the aliens are scientists. They wish to learn as much as possible about us with the least possible interference. They do this by giving one person every century special powers, and then returning for this person. I will tell them everything I know about this world, which thanks to my memory is a lot . . . '

He paused. Before us, the spaceship opened. Down the ramp waked a silver-suited alien. I wanted to turn and run, but a voice in my head told me to be calm.

As I watched, Mr Endicott walked towards the alien. They talked. Then my friend turned to me. 'Goodbye, Tommy,' he said. 'Perhaps, in time and space, we will meet again.'

Then he turned and walked quickly up the ramp into the spaceship.

The alien faced me, staring with its big black eyes behind the glass of its face-mask. I wanted to shout after Mr Endicott, ask him what he meant.

The alien reached towards me, and in its hand was a device like a pistol.

I heard a voice in my head: 'We wish you no harm, Tommy. If you, too, would like a long life on Earth, and then an even longer life among the stars . . . '

That was all it said, but it was enough.

Did I want to live for ever, it was asking? Did I want perfect health, a photographic memory, and a hundred years on Earth? Did I want to live among the stars with Mr Endicott and others like him, and the aliens?

I stepped forward and held out my hand, and the silver being touched me with the gun. I felt a warmth spread through my body, and was surrounded by light. I felt a wonderful peace which I knew would be with me for the rest of my life.

Later I watched the spaceship rise and disappear into the night sky, then turned and made my way back home.

# Activities

## The Secret of City Cemetery by Patrick Bone

1  **In a pair**, look through the story to build up a picture of where City Cemetery is and exactly how it is laid out.

Working together, draft a map of the cemetery from a bird's eye view. Include all the details mentioned in the story – e.g. Mark Twain School, the playground, the sidewalk, the open graves, the cemetery path, the grave that Willard 'haunts', and so on.

Pretend you are detectives investigating Willard's disappearance. Draw to scale a careful version of your map, using colour. Label everything that might help the investigation. This includes the last known movements of people such as the cemetery superintendent and the gravediggers.

2  Imagine Willard's body is never found. The next issue of Mark Twain School's Newsletter includes an article about him. Its headline reads:

> **MYSTERY DISAPPEARANCE OF
> MARK TWAIN STUDENT**
>
> 'Always a practical joker,' say classmates

**On your own**, write the article. You should come up with a theory about what has happened to Willard – which may or may not match the ending of the story. Include interviews with some people who knew him, such as Wylma Jean Kist and Henry Grasmick: their comments might help to back up your theory.

## **Even Stevens FC** by Michael Rosen

**1**　**In a small group**, look back to the Even Stevens team songs on pages 11–12. They are based on the players' names and characters (see pages 8–9).

Between you, make up at least three more songs/chants for the Even Stevens team. Perform them in class (a drama lesson would be ideal) after you have had time to rehearse. Afterwards, you could mount an illustrated wall display of the best ones.

**2**　The *Grandstand* report on Even Stevens' win against Blackpool ends:

'At the final whistle it was 2–1 to Even Stevens. They're into round two, and they'll be celebrating down in Hackney tonight, I can tell you.'

**On your own**, write a report of the celebrations for the back page of the *Hackney Mercury*. Make it look like a real newspaper report: include a main headline, interviews with players and fans, pictures, etc. If possible, do it on a computer.

**3**　Imagine that Even Stevens take part in a charity match against Hod's Odds, a team of ex-international players. It is televised live from Wembley a week after the Cup Final with Spurs. To try to make sure they win, Even Stevens use a new secret tactic which bends (but doesn't break) FA rules.

**In a pair**, talk about how the game might go. Imagine who will be playing for Hod's Odds. Discuss when and how Even Stevens will put their cunning plan into practice. Does it work – or does it backfire against them?

Then tape-record part of the TV commentary on the game. You can take turns to be the chief commentator and the 'expert'. In advance, write notes or a script on which to base your commentary.

# Smart Ice-Cream by Paul Jennings

1 Remind yourself of Peppi's four special ice-creams (page 27). **In a pair**, invent a kind of food (other than ice-cream) for changing someone's behaviour. It could be:

- to make bad-tempered teachers kind and patient
- to make hard cases turn soft
- to make parents treat their children with more understanding

. . . or an idea of your own.

Between you, write a recipe and cooking instructions for your food. Choose ingredients to match what the food will do to the person who eats it.

One of you should then draw a cartoon strip  showing how your chosen person behaves *before* eating. One of you should draw a cartoon strip showing how they behave *after* eating. Add speech bubbles and/or captions.

Join your cartoon strips together, with the recipe in the middle. Put them on display with others from your class.

2 Re-read the last paragraph of the story. Imagine you are the boy writing it. **On your own**, continue your account of 'the nekst day', showing how you become less and less 'smart' as time goes on.

You could describe events at home, at school, or elsewhere. What you write is up to you – but your spelling should be like that in the last paragraph.

Exchange your finished writing **with a partner**. Pretend to be your English teacher. Go through your partner's writing. First, correct about 20 of the deliberate spelling mistakes (use a dictionary where you need to). Then write a comment showing how interesting and entertaining you think the writing is.

## Just a Guess by Dick King-Smith

**1**   On television, the Nine o'clock News has a 3-minute
report about Philip's accident. A reporter presents 'to
camera' details about what happened and interviews
several people to get their reactions to the event.

**In a small group**, plan and act out this news report. Use
your knowledge of the story to make the facts accurate.
Who will be interviewed: Joe? the lorry driver? Miss
Atkinson? the police sergeant?

This activity needs to be carefully scripted for it to work
well. If you have access to a video camera, use it.

**2**   'Later on this morning we have an interesting visitor
coming in to school to talk to you' (page 29).

**On your own**, choose an 'interesting visitor' – it can be
anyone you wish – to talk to and with *your* class.

Pretend to be this person. Make notes on what you are
going to talk about. Plan answers to the questions you
think you will be asked. Then act out your 'visit' with the
rest of the class as your audience.

**3**   In newspapers and magazines, horoscopes ('Your Stars')
claim to predict the future.

**In a small group**, bring a selection of these into class.
Talk about what they say and how they are written. Why
do you think people read them? Are they just a bit of fun
– or do you take them at all seriously?

Write each other's horoscopes for the coming week.
Imitate the style of the ones you've been looking at. If
you wish, illustrate them colourfully and put them on
display.

# An Alien Stole My Brain by Maggie Powell

1   **In a small group**, talk about how the story-teller's behaviour changes when the alien invades his brain. Choose *two* really striking examples. Act them out in a drama lesson, either by improvising or by writing a script in advance. How will you make it clear to your audience that the boy is under alien control?

You could go on to imagine two other situations resulting from 'brain invasion' which are not in the story. Act them out OR combine to write about them in story form.

2   'Stop raiding my memory, there's some private stuff in there' (page 48).

Pretend that an alien has got inside the brain of one of your friends – and has access to all the 'private stuff' filed away in his/her memory.

**On your own**, write a conversation between the alien and your friend. It could begin like this:

> *Alien:*   Hey, there's some pretty uncool stuff down here. Didn't know you still take your teddy bear to bed.
>
> *Friend:*   Eh?! What are you on about?
>
> *Alien:*   Well, here you are in your Postman Pat pyjamas, holding a teddy by its ear and sucking your thumb on your way upstairs.
>
> *Friend:*   No, no, you've got it all wrong! That was at Junior School, see, when I had to be in this stupid play, and . . .
>
> *Alien:*   Expect me to believe **that**, do you?

Base the conversation on things you actually know about: it will be funnier if you do. You could tape-record (in private?) what you have written – then listen to what your friend has taped about *you*.

# Riding the Silver Wave by Ben Bo

**1**  In the story there are a number of terms surfers use to describe their sport and how to do it. **In a small group**, make a list of these, plus any others you know. Write brief, clear explanations of them for non-surfers.

Then talk about other sports and games which use special terms some young people won't understand – e.g. American football, skateboarding, BMX biking, basketball. Between you, draw up a Glossary (a list explaining uncommon words) for two or more of these. You could illustrate it and print it as a booklet.

**2**  **In a pair**, read aloud the episode in Happy Larry's café where Josh challenges Ratso to 'crack-a-can'.

What are the rules? What is the point of doing it? How is the winner decided? Talk together until you are sure you understand exactly how crack-a-can works. Then **on your own** write a 50-word description of it for someone who hasn't read this story.

**In your pair**, invent one or more *new* variations on crack-a-can, using common objects found in a classroom or in your schoolbag. Then join up with another pair. Explain and demonstrate the ideas you've come up with.

**3**  At the end of the story, Craig wins a life-saving award. Look back through the story to remind yourself of all he had done to deserve it. Briefly note down the main details.

**On your own**, write the speech which the Mayor of Cove Bay makes at Craig's award ceremony. Bear in mind that, although he might refer to Johnny-boy's death, he knows nothing about the surfer 'with the skull-face'.

# Man from the South by Roald Dahl

1   Imagine that the young American is invited to appear on a TV chat show called *You'd Never Believe It!* He is to be interviewed about his meeting with Carlos and what happened in the hotel room.

In a pair, act out the interview. You could take turns to play the chat show host and the American: swap over about half-way through. Before you start, make sure both of you know the details of the story well enough for the interview to be realistic. Tape-record it if you wish.

2   In small  group, plan a drama based on a bet between two people which turns out unexpectedly. The situation should involve at least four characters.

Act it out in a drama lesson. You can use a script or improvise – but the ending must come as a real surprise to your audience.

3   Pretend that Carlos is finally arrested for chopping off bits of his friends and neighbours. He is put on trial.

In a pair, write two speeches: one for the prosecution, and one that Carlos makes in his own defence. Use what you know from the story as a basis, but invent other details if you wish. You could round off this activity by making a tape-recording of your speeches OR by acting out as a class Carlos's trial, with witnesses, judge, jury, etc.

## Karate for Kids by Terence Blacker

**1**	Look back to page 81 where:

> 'Thirty minutes or so later, Johnson manages to reach the central desk and telephones the police.'

**In a pair**, imagine how this phone call will go, e.g:

| | |
|---|---|
| *Johnson:* | Police? This is a monster emergency! |
| *Sergeant:* | You're through to the city police department. How may I help you, sir? |
| *Johnson:* | Books! (*Ooww!*) These books are killing me! |

Script the whole phone call, which lasts about two minutes. Include some details from the story; make up others yourself. Then act it out, using suitable voices and sound-effects. Tape-record it if you wish.

**2**	'Books are people too, right?' (page 84).

**In a small group**, imagine that some books you know have an appearance and character to match their titles. (How would *The Guinness Book of Records* look, dress, speak and behave?). Make 'people drawings' of the books you choose, without giving away what they are called. Then exchange drawings with members of another group and try guessing the titles.

**On your own**, choose two of your favourite non-fiction or fiction books. Think of them as human. Imagine part of a day in their lives, during which they meet and get involved in an unusual adventure.

Tell the story of what happens to them, either as a playscript OR as a piece of prose.

**3**	**On your own**, imagine that your local library is threatened with closure – like the one in this story. Design a poster to persuade the Council to keep it open. Use whatever techniques you think will be effective.

# Gone Fishing by Jean Richardson

1   This story takes place partly in the present and partly in the past.

**In a pair**, make a Time Chart to show what is happening in the present and the past at various points in the story. Do it like this:

| Events in the present | Events in the past |
|---|---|
| 1 The Trust lady starts telling William's class the history of Bardon after they've changed into 1820s costumes. | William meets Luke and Matthew in the corridor as they are about to go fishing. |
| 2 | |

Make at least *five* entries on your chart.

When you have finished, **join up with another pair**. Compare your charts. Where there are differences, work out why by checking what you have written against the details of the story.

2   Think of somewhere *you* would enjoy visiting on either a 'Living History' or a 'Living Future' trip. It can be set in any time and be in this country or abroad. If you choose Living Future, it will, of course, be partly/completely imaginary – and you may need time travel to get there.

Pretend you are in charge of organizing school visits to wherever you have chosen. **On your own**, plan and produce an illustrated pamphlet advertising its attractions. You could do this on a computer. If you wish, also record a tape for visitors to listen to as they look round.

## **Dan, Dan the Half-Time Man** by Janet Burchett and Sara Vogler

**1**  Re-read the account of the first half between WORST FC and EViL FC (pages 104–5). It ends nil–nil.

**In a small group**, give your ideas about what might be said and done during half-time in each team's changing room. Imagine the team talks given by Chaz (WORST) and McThuggart (EViL). What plans for the second half might be hatched by EViL – especially Blades Wilkinson, Ginnie Jones and Erica the Red Card? How much will WORST be relying on Dan's sweets (despite the fact that he's missing, kidnapped)?

When you are ready, use a drama lesson to act out the half-time scene in each changing room. Try to stay true to the details and the comic mood of the story. If you wish, go on to act out highlights from the second half.

**2**  By the end of the story, Dan had become WORST FC's hero.

**In a pair**, make a large poster celebrating Dan's achievements. Include as many details from the story as you can fit in. Use a combination of words and pictures. Mount a class display of 'Dan Posters'.

**3**  Imagine that the team you play for, or support, hits on a 'winning formula' that has nothing to do with football tactics. It could, for example, involve the team's kit, their supporters, the goalposts, pitch markings, hypnotism . . . and so on. You decide.

**On your own**, describe a game where the winning formula is a brilliant success. Produce either a written match report OR a tape-recorded commentary.

# The Amazing Mr Endicott by Eric Brown

1   Re-read the account of Mr Endicott's first meeting with the aliens. It runs from 'Where did I get to, Tommy?' (page 113) to ' . . . I was surrounded by light' (page 115).

   **In a pair**, pretend you are in charge of filming this story. Discuss how you would film the scene above. Then make sketches to guide the film's director. Label them to make all the details clear. Write brief instructions for the cameraman, the sound technician and the actors.

2   Imagine that Tommy has lived to be a hundred. It is towards the end of the twenty-first century. The alien scientists are about to 'collect' Tommy so he can tell them how life on Earth has progressed.

   Put yourself in Tommy's place. What do you think you will have to report about the twenty-first century? **On your own**, jot down a few ideas. Concentrate on things that particularly interest you. You could cover: technology, war, travel, the environment, space exploration, sport etc. Explain the way things will have changed between now and then.

   **In class discussion**, share the ideas you've come up with. See if you can make an agreed list of 'The ten biggest changes to Life on Earth in the twenty-first century'.

   Now form **a small group**. Take ONE of the 'changes' on your class list. Write an illustrated report about it, looking back over the twenty-first century. You could print the finished product in the form of a booklet. If you wish, also make a tape-recording for Tommy to take with him to the aliens.

# Out of the Darkness

By Nigel Hinton

Liam and Leila are born at the same moment, thousands of miles apart.

Liam is unwanted and unloved. Leila is loved by many. But they are linked by destiny. When evil killers seek Leila, only Liam can help. Their friendship will change their lives for ever.

What is the mystery behind Leila? Liam knows he must protect her, but is he prepared for the final shocking truth?

**Lancashire Children's Book Award Winner**

**Age 12+    ISBN: 0 435 12500 1**

# Music on the Bamboo Radio

By Martin Booth

*If the enemy catch him, they'll kill him . . .*

Nicholas Holford is smuggled to safety
in China when Japan invades Hong Kong in
1941. Not knowing if his parents are alive
or dead, he must pretend to be Chinese.
If the enemy discovers he is European,
he will not survive.

Then Nicholas joins the secret fight against
the Japanese. He learns about explosives,
but also about 'music on the bamboo radio'
– smuggling information to prisoner-of-war
camps. It is dangerous and deadly. But
when only Nicholas can help, he chooses to
take the risk . . .

**Age 12+    ISBN: 0 435 12490 0**

# Chandra

By Frances Mary Hendry

*Her grandmother was anxious.
'Jaisalmer is a long-long way off.
Away out in the desert. Nineteen hours
by train. And then on to a farm twenty
kilometres further yet. If anything
goes wrong –'*

Chandra's grandmother is anxious about
Chandra's marriage to a boy who lives far
away in the deserts of Rajasthan. But no
one listens to her concerns and soon
Chandra finds that her life is to change
dramatically . . .

**Age 12+   ISBN: 0 435 12519 2**

Martha is different. She longs to have friends
and to be accepted by her class-mates. But
her parents belong to a strict religious
group. They have rules that mean
no computers, no TV, no trendy clothes
. . . and no friends.

Martha also has a secret. Its name is
Abomination and it must never be
discovered. But when Scott makes friends
with Martha, she has a choice to make.
Should she tell him about her terrible
secret?

**Age 12+    ISBN: 0 435 12510 9**

# The best in classic and

Jane Austen

Elizabeth Laird

Beverley Naidoo        Roddy Doyle

Robert Swindells

George Orwell

Charles Dickens

Charlotte Brontë

Jan Mark

Anne Fine

Anthony Horowitz